"CITIZENS OF ROMA"
Written by Jameson Flynn
Edited by Dara Schechter

Citizens of Roma, is a work of fiction based on real people, actual places and historical events.

Copyright Jameson Flynn/Shiloh Press
January 2017
First Edition Published May 2018

Special Thanks :
Page Layout --Francois Granger CREAPRINT
Cover Design--Rachel Simone
Online Editor--Olivia Shiloh
Contributing Editor—Susan O'Grady

ISBN 978-0-9738149-4-1

For them that was and those to come...JF

# CITIZENS OF ROMA

# CITIZENS

## of

## Roma

### BY

## JAMESON FLYNN

And miracles to make before I sleep...
-Ivan Ambrose Goddinski

# FALL OF ROMA

Can't tell by looking at her now but this town used to be something special, a real shining star. People would move here from all over, from other countries even, just to live the good life, to raise their kids in this safe, beautiful town blessed with gold-medal schools, pure drinking water and clean mountain air. Seems like it wasn't even that long ago when everything was working the way it should. Our classrooms were filled with happy, good-looking, healthy, smart kids, and Roma's teams were winning all the championships. Our stores and businesses were packed with customers; you had to wait in line to buy a house, because nobody was selling theirs. Roma was the place to be, the best town to live in Vermont, in New England, hell, in the whole country and probably the entire world. That was then, before the unravelling of everything Roma stood for, before our way of life lost its way.

Seems like everyone who moved here for that good life has moved away these past few years, almost like it happened overnight. We just woke up one day and they were gone, leaving behind most of their furniture, shaggy front lawns and blown down For Sale signs. Where did they go? I don't even know. Florida probably, lots of people choose Florida. I guess they like the muggy weather and Winnebago-sized flying bugs.

Maybe it's those Early Bird Specials where you can eat dinner at three o'clock in the afternoon for ten bucks and then go home and drink yourself to sleep. The Indians used to call

Florida "Swamp Hell," the place they sent you when you weren't alive anymore. Sounds about right to me.

I heard on the news that lots of people are moving into these gated communities where everything you need is delivered, and you can't get in or out without a pass code and a DNA sample. We've got one of those security gates up on the mountain and most of those folks have moved out too. It's only about half-full now because families who couldn't afford their payments anymore ended up getting evicted, or just disappeared into the night.

"Are you kids going to buy anything, or just go around touching stuff?"

They look at me like I'm the asshole, but they've been in here for almost an hour, just like yesterday and all the days before. I know they have no money to spend. Nobody does anymore. It's not even two o'clock in the afternoon, they should still be in school.  Instead, these little goons are running all over town, with my store their first stop.

My family opened Reardon's General Store almost a hundred and fifty years ago, just after the Civil War. We weren't the first business here, but our little general store is today the oldest business still standing in Roma. I can't figure out if that's good or bad, but it does explain why I feel like I can never leave this town. Roma's in my blood, she's who I am. When everyone else picks up and leaves, it's always the townies, the people who built it in the first place who remain. Once we leave, it's all over, the fat lady's sung her final song. Say what you will about townies, but we are loyal to where we grew up, loyal to our family history, loyal to who we are. Truth is, we really don't have much of a choice.

"Rufus, are you going to the town meeting tonight?"

Katie Konklin, the love of my life, jolts me from my juvenile delinquent surveillance. How long has she been standing there? Was I talking to myself again?

"I'm sorry, Katie, I was watching those kids. Every time they come in things disappear, entire shelves go bare. Town meeting, is that tonight? Oh yeah, it's Wednesday. Sure, I'll be there. What else am I going to do for entertainment on a weeknight in Roma? Maybe Stringer will bring along his monkey again. I hate that monkey."

"Don't worry about the monkey. I think they told Stringer that Bubba wasn't welcome back. But you never know, Stringer's a little hard of hearing since he blew up his snowmobile engine."

"Stringer hears just fine. He just lets Bubba do whatever he wants. The two of them are inconsiderate to others."

"See you tonight then, Rufus." Katie Konklin walks out past the boys who watch her from behind the magazine rack. The biggest kid is Billy Burkenstock, a heavyset manchild wearing his hat backwards. He makes a joke only his gang can hear and they all start laughing, probably at Katie's expense. That does it, I've had enough.

"Okay boys time's up. If you're not going to buy anything then it's time to move on to your next hangout. Did school get out early today, again?"

"Yes sir, Mr. Reardon. We only had a half day." The other kids laugh as Billy grabs a carton of teriyaki beef jerky and comes to the counter. I swear he's put on ten pounds and grown three inches since yesterday. He's growing abnormally. The kid's a behemoth. At seventeen, he's already six foot six and at least three-hundred pounds. Billy

Burkenstock used to be an all-star soccer player known for his speed. He was Roma's best goal scorer, a real striker. Now he's a shoplifter, and a pretty bad one at that.

"How much is the jerky, Mr. Reardon?"

"Same as yesterday and the day before that, Billy. Three dollars a pack, thirty dollars for the carton. You going to buy some today, Billy?" He's so big I can't even see the other kids standing behind him. It strikes me, that's probably his plan.

"Nah, that's just too expensive for me. Why do they charge so much for jerky? It's just dried up beef. See you tomorrow, Mr. Reardon." Billy leaves the beef jerky on the counter and walks out into the falling snow, followed by his gang of the cackling four.

Everyone in Roma comes here. They have to, I'm the only general store in town and for ten miles beyond. We carry everything a general store should. All the other stores are specialty shops, which in the end is what kills them. It's better to be the generalist. Plus, I've got the four gas pumps and sooner or later everyone needs gas. The three meeting places in Roma are my store, the town dump, and of course, Grady's Pub. I guess you could also count the town meeting, but not as many people show up there anymore. They figure what's the point, what's done is done.

Roma's town meetings used to be packed with people who wanted to voice their ideas for making our town even better. Back then, people listened to each other with respect. We had a real sense of community—folks truly cared about Roma, about each other, about where we were headed. I believe that all changed five years ago, when the money dried up and families just moved away without so much as a goodbye wave and a nice knowing you farewell. That's when people started acting desperate and being disrespectful. It's when Roma began her decline into this decaying ruin of broken dreams and abandoned ambitions she's become today.

I spot Henry Huntington, filling up his BMW at pump number one outside my window. Henry's the last of our local trust funders. He never worked a day in his life and he's proud of it, even boasts about it. Most of the trust funders, and we used to have a bunch living here in Roma because trust funders love to ski, most of them try to hide their inherited wealth, pretending they have a job somewhere else, or that they made their money in the stock market. That's always a good one because you can't really trace it, and any idiot can make money in the stock market. Many have.

Henry Huntington used to come back to Roma four months out of every year. He'd come here to ski with his trust fund buddies. But lately Roma's weather and ski conditions haven't been up to snuff for Henry and his friends who have migrated west these past few years to hit the slopes and spend their inherited money. He's back in town to try and sell his family's home. It's a huge place sitting on top of the mountain looking down on Roma, just like Henry does. It has ten bedrooms, ten bathrooms and ten fireplaces to match. Who's going to buy it? Henry's going to have to take twenty-five cents on the dollar just to get an offer. Poor Henry. I knock on the window and wave my middle finger at him. He throws me both middle fingers back, and even keeps one held in the air as he drives off in his brand new Beamer. It's our little way of saying hello, goodbye, and what we truly feel about each other all at the same time. More people should do it, like they do in Italy.

Roma sits on a windy mountain road that climbs all the way up to our state's highest peak, which makes us a natural ski destination when conditions are right. We used to be the best place to ski on the East Coast. All the beautiful people and famous skiers came to Roma to party and ski, and then party some more. That was before all the weather patterns shifted with global warming, and all the good snowstorms veered to the west. These days it seems like winter never ends, and not in a good way. Now we get mostly freezing rain followed by subzero bitter cold, followed by massive blizzards that last three or four days and drop way too much snow to groom or even run the chairlifts. Not ideal conditions for skiing, or for partying in Roma. So we don't see much of Henry and his crowd anymore.

Katie Konklin has always been the best-looking girl in Roma. We grew up together, lived near each other, went through school and graduated the same year. She was my beautiful girl next door, even though she lived a few houses down, and one block over. Katie was the girl I always wanted to date but never had the guts to ask. Then she moved away, and I stayed right here in Roma. But like all us townies, you just can't stay away from who you really are for too long. Katie moved back to Roma about three years ago and I couldn't be happier. The only real reason I even go to these town meetings anymore is to see Katie, socially. Otherwise, they are a giant waste of time where people call each other names and blame Roma's downfall on the other guy. Sometimes fights break out and chairs get thrown. Those meetings I like. Katie and I just sit in the back, eating her chocolate chip cookies she always bakes for the meeting, and we just enjoy the show. It's reality community theatre, kind of scary but really funny to watch.

There's Billy Burkenstock and his motley crew coming out of the bowling alley now. That's record time for them getting tossed. Only that bunch could get thrown out of a bowling alley. Billy and his cohorts have become the lost boys of Roma over these past few years. They wander around town looking for a place to be, never wanting to go home. Everyone knows it's these boys who have been setting the bonfires up the mountain road, letting them burn wild until our police and firemen show up to put them out. The boys never seem to be around when the cops finally arrive on the scene. But we know it's them. That's one good thing about living in a small town that's getting even smaller by the day, there are never too many suspects, just the usual ones.

Watching Billy and his wild boys I'm reminded of my own high school days, so very different from what theirs seem to be. I loved going to school, playing sports, feeling like I was a part of something special. We were the Roma Centurions and damn proud of it. I was on every team; not that I was any good but in a Division III small town like Roma every kid got to play varsity, maybe even score a goal or two for their high school glory moments. I had three goals in my varsity soccer career. Two of them were the very first goals scored by our team in my junior and senior seasons, which turned out to be undefeated championship seasons. Those goals are my very own small claim to Roma fame.

Billy and his crew never knew those moments. By the time they reached the varsity level there weren't even enough kids to field a full team, and all the good coaches had retired or left town. I feel a bit of sadness watching them wander aimlessly from place to place. Maybe they're searching for the lost girls of Roma. They'll never find them. The girls are too smart. They just stay at home, counting down the days until they can leave Roma for the big city, like everyone else.

I don't look much like an athlete anymore, that's for sure, not even close. With my long graying hair and full winter beard, I resemble one of those chubby yard gnomes. I think I was destined to be a fat guy. My mom told me too many times that when I was born Doctor Carson told her I was already heavy for my height and that she shouldn't feed me too much breast milk. Imagine that, being deprived of breast milk. Who does that to a baby? I think that's why I'm always so thirsty. I was barely out of the womb and they already had me on a diet. Of course I was screaming all the time. I was thirsty for the nipple and being denied my right to nourishment. These days I weigh in at about two-hundred-fifty pounds. I'm barely five foot eight, so I look like a square block, a bearded Rubik's Cube wearing glasses and a hat.

I strongly believe we fat people are misunderstood by everyone else. What folks don't get is that fat is our protective layer against all the horror and disappointments of the world we live in. Not just in Roma but everywhere.

People need to feel good about themselves and the lives they lead, if only for a brief moment in their day. Some people, like me, we eat too much. Others drink or smoke too much. Some use drugs, others use sex. It almost doesn't matter which vice you choose, it's all the same. As they used to say when this town was something special...all roads lead to Roma. These days, all roads lead to instant gratification, because that's the only good feeling you're going to get, even if it is fleeting. In my case, and many others, it's all about the food, and plenty of it. Never once have I been rejected by a big bowl of pasta or some barbecued ribs. We live in a world today where most people are excluded from just about everything...jobs, sports, clubs, even relationships...only the chosen few or the well-connected get to participate. Food says to everyone, come on in, you're invited, let's party. There's plenty for everyone and more in the kitchen. When you're full, we're rolling out dessert. Food doesn't care what you look like, who you're related to, how big your bank account is, or where you come from. Food is that friend who is always there and ready to eat. I say, thank God for food. As life choices go, it turns out to be the safest, definitely the tastiest.

A high-pitched squeal calls me back from thinking about food and watching the lost boys from my storefront window perch. It's Harry Hancock the Mayor of Babylon, our neighboring town just ten miles away. Babylon is an old mill town built on a river bank and surrounded by three small lakes. Everyone from Roma, and all the other small towns in this area, used to pack a lunch, sometimes dinner too, and drive to Babylon to spend the day swimming, fishing and waterskiing with family and friends. In the winter, ice-fishing was the best. Those were great days for Babylon. But ever since that bus accident ten years back, nobody seems to spend family time in Babylon anymore. These days Babylon is just another dying town with only a few folks left; it's as if they're cursed and can never leave the scene of their crime. But Harry is the mayor, for better or worse. He always has been and probably always will be. He smoked so much when he was a kid he got throat cancer in his thirties. Ever since, Harry needs to hold one of those microphones to his larynx just to speak.

9

"Give me two packs of Marlboro and six lotto tickets, Rufus; and a couple of Red Bulls for the ride home."

"Haven't seen you for a while, Harry. How's things going in Babylon?"

"Same as always, Rufus. Not much going on. Got plenty of shacks out there for the ice-fishing but it's mostly locals. You fishing this winter? I don't think I saw you out there last year."

Harry Hancock's voice box makes him sound like a computer when he talks. It's like listening to Stephen Hawking, only without the higher intelligence.

"Nope, I haven't been out for a few years, Harry. It's too damn cold for me. These days, I like to hunker down and get cozy during the winter months. Besides, I was always afraid of breaking through the ice, not being able to climb out and nobody ever finding me."

Harry finds that image funny and laughs out loud at full volume through his microphone as he walks out of the store. "Can't be afraid of everything, Rufus, or you'll never do anything."

I open a bottle of Cabernet and slice off a few chunks of Blue Cheese for lunch. Cold weather and falling snow always makes me hungry, and you just have to drink Cabernet in the winter. I don't know how people don't...

# TOWN MEETING

"If we don't fix our covered bridge it's just going to crumble. Then what? We'll have a cover with no bridge. We'll look silly and we won't even be able to get up and down the mountain. We put all that money toward a new ice rink that hardly anybody uses but not a penny to fix our infrastructure. Roma's falling down all around us. Nobody seems to notice, or even care. Street lights don't work. The sewers are backing up after every rainstorm, and the roads have potholes the size of swimming pools."

Little Ivan stands on his chair, so everyone can hear him above all the side conversations going on. Ivan's just a little over four feet tall, thus his nickname Little Ivan. We call him that with no disrespect, it's just who he is in Roma. I used to think Ivan was a midget, but it turns out he's really a dwarf. He explained the difference to me when we were in high school together. I like Ivan. He's the smartest person in Roma, though there's not a lot of competition. It's definitely a low bar. Chester Connelly was smart too, but he died in the Fall. Chester never agreed with anyone on anything, except maybe Ivan once in a while. I have noticed over the years that what Ivan says is going to happen usually ends up happening.

"There's just not enough money to fix everything, Ivan, and you know that. Federal government is not sending any more money. They're broke too. That's why we're here tonight, not to talk about what needs fixing. First, we need to figure out a way to get more money. Then we can fix stuff. Infrastructure, are you kidding me?"

Mary Yeldir, Roma's mayor, sits on the stage above the crowd looking down on the people, who are mostly milling around the dessert table not listening to her. Mayor Mary likes to pound her gavel when things start getting too out of hand, as they always do, so she starts pounding away as everyone talks even louder. I'm sitting next to Katie enjoying the chaos and eating my fourth cookie. I don't really care what anybody is saying. I'm with Katie and life is good. It's these little moments you need to capture and appreciate to feel truly happy in this life.

Little Ivan and Mayor Mary always go at it in our town meetings which used to draw a lot more people, up to five hundred sometimes. These days we're lucky if fifty of Roma's finest citizens show up. Even then, it's mostly for the free dessert, maybe to go out for a drink or two afterward at Grady's Pub.

Our little town meeting used to be quite the hotspot for hooking up. Where else are you going to meet people around here? Maybe the town dump, everyone goes there at least once a week. Ivan says there are so many rats at the dump now they're starting to invade the town. I have seen a few out back of the store lately and noticed they're getting bigger and bolder every week. At least the rats are doing well.

"See what I mean, Rufus? You just can't miss a town meeting. They're such fun, like a soap opera, only you actually know all the characters. Look, over by the coat rack, there's Mitzi and Jack all over each other again."

Katie has a special radar for spotting hookups even before they happen. She knew Mitzi and Jack were going to get together about a year ago. Mitzi Clark's husband left her with three daughters. Jack Adam's wife walked out on him about the same time, leaving behind their two sons. Hmmm. Put them together and they have the makings of a starting five basketball team, just saying.

Like Roma, our town meeting is a dying animal. I remember what these meetings used to be–everyone happy to see each other, everyone listening to each other's point of view no matter how out there it might have been. These days it's just sniping, blaming, bickering, talking about how bad things are and how it's getting even worse. Nobody has any big ideas that are going to make things better anymore, including me. I'm an optimist most of the time but I can't figure how things get better from here. Roma is in her dark ages and I just don't see a light at the end of this tunnel.

Chief Ridley gets a call on his radio saying someone, and we all know who, has set a fire off the mountain road above town. Chief's radio is always turned up just loud enough so everyone in the meeting can hear the call along with him, even with all the noise. He leaves immediately with three volunteer firemen to go put out the flames and look for the piros, who they never do seem able to find.

Ivan's on his chair again. "It's the kids doing it. Everyone knows it, doesn't take a detective, or even our police chief to figure that out. Why doesn't Chief Ridley just arrest them before every town meeting? That will put an end to "FireGate." The room goes completely silent as everyone considers Ivan's solution. When Ivan speaks, people always listen. I remember a few years back, Ivan was the first to notice how all the rich families were moving away from Roma. He said that's never a good sign when the money leaves town.

I can hear young Samantha Strange playing her fiddle outside town hall. Samantha's a young kid, maybe seventh or eighth grade but she plays a mean fiddle. She taught herself to play, which is impressive. Cute kid, a little odd how she's always talking to herself between songs, but we all love to hear Samantha play her fiddle. Everyone in the Strange family played an instrument. Samantha is a prodigy from a family of prodigies. At every town meeting you'll find Samantha set up outside, filling the night air with beautiful music, as we all file past dropping dollars and coins into her fiddle case. I swear the kid rakes it in. She's good and she knows it. I love it when people know they're good at something and want to share their gift with others. To me that's high art, and they are the true artists.

The meeting's heating up. Mayor Mary is pounding her gavel so hard now, you can see little pieces of wood splintering off every time she bangs it. Mitzi is on top of Jack on the floor behind the coat rack; they're going at it full-throttle. Ivan's standing tippy-toed on his chair saying how we must merge our schools with the neighboring towns because we just don't have enough students or teachers anymore.

Then, over in the corner by the back door exit I spot him. It's Stringer with his crazy monkey Bubba. They must have snuck in. Even worse, Bubba sees me at the same time and we lock eyes. Never, ever lock eyes with a crazy monkey, they take it as a challenge. I can't look away fast enough. Now Bubba's showing me his teeth as he jumps off Stringer's shoulder and starts hip-hopping on people's heads, making his way across the room, toward me.

I hear Samantha Strange playing, "Ode to Joy" as I take Katie Konklin's hand and make a desperate lurch for the door, grabbing for one last chocolate chip cookie as we move past the dessert table. As it turns out, that extra cookie is my fatal mistake. That one brief detour gives Bubba just enough time to cut off my angle to our escape route. He's perched in a death crouch on Little Ivan's head, staring right at me, and I swear he's smiling. He takes off from Ivan like a flying monkey and leaps toward me from what must be ten feet away. Seeing him airborne, I do the only gentlemanly thing I can think of; I shove Katie toward the door to save her from Bubba, momentarily forgetting about the dessert table between us and the exit. Katie lands face first on a Boston cream pie knocking over the entire table, as Bubba makes a hard landing, feet first on my head. I feel a warm, steady stream coming from Bubba who is screeching and beating his chest. Samantha's fiddle plays, *"Somewhere Over the Rainbow"* outside, and I remember thinking 'good movie, Judy Garland', as I scream across the room, "Get your crazy monkey off my head, Stringer. Bubba's pissing on me again."

Looking down at Katie covered in chocolate and pie and other baked goods, I see she's laughing with tears running down her Boston cream cheeks. At least I saved her from Bubba, sort of. Stringer finally gets over to me and grabs Bubba from my head, but not before Bubba gives me one final squirt as we separate.

"This is exactly why I don't like coming to town meetings anymore. Stuff like this never used to happen in Roma because we never let crazy monkeys in," I say to Katie as I help her up from the floor. She's still laughing. I'm pretty sure it's at me because I'm not laughing, so it's not with me.

Mayor Mary pounds her final gavel as the town meeting is adjourned over to Grady's Pub, Roma's last remaining watering hole. I'm seriously thinking of skipping next week's town meeting, even if Katie is going to be there with her delicious cookies.  It's just too dangerous...

## EVERYBODY'S HOME NOW

I love the holidays, especially when it's snowing like this. Pulling the covers up over my head and listening to the wind blowing through the trees makes me feel so cozy, warm and safe in my bed. It's way too early for me to go to sleep. I like to lay awake late as I can and wait for them to come home. One by one they do you know. We're always together for the holidays, just like we promised.

Usually it's my brother Sebastian who shows up first. He tries to sneak into my room just like when we were kids. But I always caught him back then and I still catch him, even though he's a lot quieter now. Seb went away to college a few years ago. It seems like so long since he left, but college is only four years. He wants to be a doctor so all he does anymore is read big books. Sebastian says coming home for the holidays is his favorite thing to do.

"Boo. Got you, Sammy. You never even heard me coming."

"How did you get in? I swear I didn't hear the door open and I was listening for it too. It's so good to see you, Sebastian. I really miss you. Where's my hug?"

"Right here…maybe if you didn't have your head buried under the covers you might have noticed me over by the windows. But I am getting pretty good at this suddenly appearing stuff. If I can get past my little sister, Samantha, everyone else will be a piece of cake. Look at you, you're getting so big."

"I was just thinking about you Seb, how you're always the first one to arrive."

"Yes, I know. I could feel you...you're my little sister, Sam, we're connected forever. Your thoughts are my thoughts, when you're thinking about me it's because I'm thinking about you at the same time. Now, where's Mom and Dad?"

"They're driving home...I mean they're not here yet. But they'll be here soon. You know Mom will start balling when she sees you. What did you bring me?"

"Who says I brought you anything, kid. Maybe I forgot this time. You know it's not easy carrying stuff all this way."

"Alright fine, maybe I don't have anything for you either. Maybe I do, maybe I don't...I can't even remember."

"Tell you what Sammy, I'll go get unpacked, put a few things away, and I just might have a special something for you. Maybe I will, maybe I won't...there's just no telling on a night like this. Now pull those covers back over your enormous head and watch this."

Sebastian throws my comforter over me, and by the time I pop my head out he's already gone. I can hear him down the hallway in his room moving things around. I wonder what he brought me. Last year it was my red beret all the way from Paris. I wear it every time I play my fiddle around town. People love it. I hear someone down in the kitchen and know right away it's Uncle Bruno. His first stop is always the kitchen to make a sandwich even before he comes upstairs to say hello. Uncle Bruno is a sergeant in the Marines. He's been a Marine, and a sergeant now that I think about it, ever since I can remember. He's my Dad's older brother and he always comes home for the holidays, no matter how far away he is. I creep down the stairs and sneak into the

18

kitchen to surprise attack him. Without even turning, he knows I'm there.

"Hello, Samantha, I heard you on the first step. Where's the mustard? You gotta have mustard in this house. It's not really a sandwich without the mustard. I can't even believe it. I travel all this way and there's no mustard for Uncle Bruno. This is my worst nightmare, Samantha."

Uncle Bruno has one of those booming voices that carry throughout the whole house. He calls it his sergeant's voice. Even though I'm standing right in front of him, he's speaking so loud I could hear him all the way upstairs. Mom says he never learned an inside voice, and his ears don't work like they used to because of all the explosions he's been so close to.

"Well look at you, Samantha, even more beautiful than last year. March right over here and give your tired Uncle Bruno a bear hug. Then please find me some mustard. I'm starving to death here."

We both laugh because Uncle Bruno never looks like he's starving to death in his uniform that always looks too small and way too tight on him. I wonder why he's still a sergeant. After all these years he probably should be a general at least. I find the mustard on the side of the refrigerator door right behind the barbecue sauce. Uncle Bruno grunts "Oorah!" and gives me a salute.

"Thank you, Sammy Sue. You just keep coming through every year saving old Sergeant Bruno's life. I think you found the mustard for me last year too, and the year before that. Who's here besides us?"

"Sebastian's upstairs in his bedroom settling in. He arrived just before you."

"He always does. That's because I have so much further to travel. I'm stationed on the other side of midnight when these holidays get here. But nothing can stop me from coming home to see you and the family, Sammykins."

"Did you see? I baked fudge-nut brownies for you, Uncle Bruno. Well, they're really for everyone, but mostly for you because I know how much you like them. I miss you. I miss you all so much, every single day. I wish it wasn't just the holidays when I get to see you and be together like this."

"But you know we're always with you, Sam. Oh yeah, these are delicious. Who knew you could bake, kid?"

"You did for one. I make them every year and you eat most of them."

Suddenly we hear piano music coming from the living room. It's the Boogie-Woogie Honky-Tonk Shuffle, and I know who's playing it. My brother Emmett is home. He always goes straight for the piano; like Uncle Bruno goes to the kitchen.

"Oh, I forgot to tell you, Sam, Emmett's home too. We arrived together. Didn't travel together, we just arrived at the same time. I turned around and there he was. Think of the odds. Go ahead. I'm gonna finish my sandwich and then find me some milk to go with these brownies."

"Try to leave some for everyone else. Love you, Uncle Bruno."

"I know you do, kid...feel it all the time, wherever I am."

Sneaking up on Emmett is the easiest. He's forever lost in his music, always playing his Boogie-Woogie bass keys leaving the high notes open for me. I jump right in, tapping the A-keys, keeping pace with Emmett's lower rhythm, just like when we were kids trying to sound like Jerry Lee Lewis himself.

"We still got it, SamStar. Watch this, kiddo."

Emmett stands up, turns around and keeps playing with his hands behind his back without looking or even missing a note, just like crazy Jerry Lee does it. I keep playing, but I can't stop laughing.

"I think you've gotten even better, Sam. Have you been performing without me?

"Like I even have a choice. Good to have you home, Emmett."

"Good to be back."

"Your hair's so long. Uncle Bruno calls you my hippie brother and says you need a haircut, a marine haircut like his."

I look over and see Uncle Bruno watching us from the kitchen. He suddenly turns his head toward the patio widows. Standing just outside the French doors watching us play, I can see my sister Gina covered in snow. How long has she been there? I run to the door and let her in.

"Welcome home, Dr. Gina. Would you like to come in from the snow and maybe join us? I'm sure it's a bit warmer in here."

"First, you step outside, give your big sister a hug and take in these beautiful stars. Oh, how I've missed you, Samantha. Now look at those two, somebody has to stop that right away."

Inside, Uncle Bruno and Sebastian are doing a swing dance to Emmett's Boogie-Woogie shuffle. They're actually pretty good, considering they're both trying to lead.

"We better go cut in before they start trying to tango. Where does the time go, Samantha? Seems like it was just a moment ago since I saw you last year. You're growing up so beautifully. You are going to play your fiddle for us tonight, aren't you?"

"Just try and stop me. I brought down your guitar from the attic. Why does it always end up back in the attic, every year? Sebastian's trumpet is in his room, and Uncle Bruno's saxophone is next to the piano just where he left it. Tonight, we all play together again, like we used to...The Strange Family Band Reunion."

Gina taps Uncle Bruno on the shoulder and dances away with Sebastian. Uncle Bruno bows, reaches for my hand and spins me around as Emmett plays his Boogie-Woogie shuffle faster and better than ever. It feels so good to have everybody together again, if only for the holidays. Well, almost everyone. When Mom and Dad get home, everything will be perfect. Looking outside, I notice it's snowing even heavier now.

I think I see lights outside in the driveway. When I run over and open our front door nobody is out there; no car is in the driveway. But I swear I saw lights. Emmett stops playing and everyone sprawls out on the couch.

"Don't worry, Satchmo, they'll be here. Besides, you're always safe with us, they know that. Uncle Bruno reaches out and pulls me to the couch."

We all lay in silence, listening to the wind howl outside as the snow falls in what has become a heavy blizzard. I can't even see outside the windows anymore as the snow covers over the glass. We are getting snowed in. I keep thinking about Mom and Dad trying to get home.

The flames dance in the fireplace in harmony with the wind outside. I always love our family fires, when we sit close together watching a movie, feeling the warmth and pure enjoyment of being with each other. It was Sebastian who taught me that no two fires are ever the same. Each fire has its own original look and design. He's right. Over these past few years, I've been taking photos of our family fires and they never look alike. Not even a little.

"I remember when we had that fire in my dorm my freshman year."

Sebastian gets up to poke the coals and throw on another log as the flames dance even higher. I can feel the fire's heat enveloping me like my warmest quilt. We are all aglow in its golden radiance.

"Turns out some idiot left a hot plate or curling iron plugged in late that night. They fell asleep and the term paper they were working on caught fire. Then their drapes caught fire, and before you knew it our whole hallway was ablaze. I was sound asleep. It was almost three in the morning, when somebody started shaking me. Chaz, my roommate, says we need to go outside right now. The entire dorm building was on fire. I thought it was a dream at first, the way everyone was walking around in their pajamas. It was eerie. I remember stumbling toward the only light I could see through all the flames and smoke at the end of the hallway. It was the red lit EXIT sign."

Suddenly there I was, there we all were, standing outside in whatever clothes we could grab, which made for some rather odd outfits. I was standing next to Chaz who had ash all over his face, and we were watching our dormitory burn down. I have to say, it made a beautiful bonfire blazing high up into the sky. You would have wanted to snap a picture Sammy, probably a few because it was so big. Funny thing was, it was snowing that night too. Not a blizzard like this one but snowing pretty good. I was standing outside in my bare feet and didn't feel cold, not even a little bit. I thought maybe the fire's heat was keeping everyone warm enough not to feel frozen. Nobody spoke. We all just stood there in silence for what seemed like a long time but may have been just a few minutes. It was such a beautiful night. The stars looked closer than usual, like you could reach up and touch them. I think I actually did touch one of them.

I see more lights flickering outside our front windows. I jump up and open the door, but again nobody is out there, just gusting wind driving endless snow. Uncle Bruno opens a bottle of my dad's good red wine, vin rouge as he likes to call it. He pours me a small glass, like he does every year.

"C'mon, Sammy Doo, you know there's no place we'd rather be tonight than right here with you, waiting for your Mom and Dad to come home. Here's to family. Here's to being together, forever and ever."

Sebastian raises his glass, "Always and forever, we're the Strange family, you just can't get rid of us, Sammy." We all clink our glasses. The wine feels warm with a taste of berry. I like it. Uncle Bruno goes into the kitchen and returns with the plate of brownies I put out. I notice half of them are already gone. "Umm, brownies and vin rouge. Now it's a party. Look up at the ceiling, Sammy."

The fire's glow is lighting up the living room ceiling like a big movie screen. I can see our shadows cast perfectly by the fire's flames. Uncle Bruno starts waltzing. He looks like a big bear dancing  on our shadow theater stage.

"Funny how it's just a handful of moments that stay with you. No matter what happens or wherever you go, you always keep those big moments, Sammy, the ones that made a difference in your journey."

Uncle Bruno isn't dancing anymore. He looks even bigger than usual, larger than life standing in front of us with the fire burning brilliantly behind him. The logs must have shifted; I can't see his shadow on the ceiling anymore, but his voice is loud and clear like always.

"Seems wherever they send us, it's always so hot, over one hundred degrees hot. I hate the heat. This snow is more my kind of weather. All I can think of when we're out on patrol is, why would anyone want to live here anyway, and why do we have to defend it? If we could just have the next war up in the Arctic, that would be wonderful. All the soldiers would be a lot happier. I know I would. Even the officers would like it, and they're never happy about anything."

"I can remember being in Afghanistan, way up in the mountains in the middle of nowhere. We were on digger patrol, that's what they call it when you're retrieving bodies from a firefight that already happened. No man left behind means somebody's got to go back and get them. I could tell right away this was a bad area, nothing but big rocks and hidden caves up there. It's always the caves you need to watch out for. Bad guys with big guns love their caves. Just as I'm about to take some water, there's a hundred guys shooting at us from behind those rocks and from the caves way up above us. We walked right into an ambush. It's a hundred and ten degrees and I haven't eaten anything but a candy bar for two days. Now I'm getting shot at by guys I can't even see. Oh, and I'm almost out of ammo too. What did I do, you might ask?"

"What did you do, Uncle Bruno, what did you do?"

"Thanks for asking, Sarsaparilla. I went full mental is what I did. I took my mind to a tropical island with a nice cool breeze blowing on a white sandy beach. It might have been Bali. I was there once and can still remember the topless native girls serving me ice cold drinks all day long. I visualized myself standing in the crystal-clear water drinking a Pina Colada, heavy on the rum, thinking this couldn't be more perfect. Then I conjured that same beach sitting just on the other side of those rocks they were shooting at us from. We only had to make it a few hundred yards to where the choppers would be waiting to get us the hell out of there. Like a plough horse making for his corral at the end of a long day, I charged forward like it was dinner time. I had to make it to those choppers and nothing was going to stop me. I said, "See you on the other side boys." Then I loaded my reserve clip, threw my last two smoke grenades and ran like one of those Pamplona bulls straight at those rocks, firing everything I had left. The rest of my guys followed right behind me. I was their lead blocker, their very own Bronko Nagurski, the greatest fullback of all time, and we were making that chopper."

"That's how I won these two medals. They say I saved my whole platoon that day, when all I was doing was trying to get to a beach that wasn't really there. Next thing I can remember, I'm on a chopper heading back to base and everyone's looking at me funny. I was all shot up, so they kept sticking me with morphine hits which made me loopy. Don't you know, I woke up on that paradise island drinking a Pina

Colada recovering from my wounds...now I'm here with all of you. See, Samantha, it's only those  handful of moments that matter, not all the in-betweens. It all works out in the end, just never the way you think it's gonna."

"Wow, Uncle Bruno, that's better than a movie. You're a true hero."

"Nah, just a soldier, Samantha. Just a tired, old soldier."

Uncle Bruno throws more logs on the fire.

"No matter how far away we get, all roads lead us back to you, Samantha."

"Me too, Sammy, seems like I'm always driving home from someplace far away to get back here. I remember how a few years ago I had just left Boston heading out to Denver."

"I forget, Emmett, why were you moving all the way out to Denver?"

"Same reason everyone moves to Denver, Sammy, to start over, to begin again. My job ended just like that. I come in one day and the club owner says he doesn't need me to play piano anymore, he's going with a DJ. No warning or anything, just that's it, you're all done. I go home to tell my girlfriend what happened, and she says she's breaking up with me. She was looking for a good time to tell me, and to her, this very shitty day seemed like a good time to tell me. When I asked her why she was breaking up with me, she said she thinks I love playing piano more than I love playing her. She did have a point; since the apartment was in her name and she paid most of the rent anyway, I was evicted. She had all my bags packed and ready to go, waiting for me outside the door. Now this all happened in the space of about two hours. It wasn't even lunch time yet. The only thing I had left in my life that was still mine was my car."

"The old black Lincoln. I remember that car. You used to give me rides to school in it. I'd sit in the back and you'd wear a hat like you were my chauffeur. All the Roma kids were jealous."

"That's the one, Sammy, my '64 Lincoln with those suicide doors, a classic. The only car I ever owned. I loved that car. They made them with so much style back then, real leather on those seats too. Not like the canvas and fake leather they use now. I figured what the hell, there's nothing holding me in Boston anymore, that's for damn sure. I'm moving to Denver. I knew a girl out there, and she played a pretty mean guitar. We could make some beautiful music together, maybe even start a band. So just like that I closed my bank account, all eleven-hundred and fifty dollars of it, threw my stuff in the trunk, those old Lincoln's have huge trunks, and I was on the road just before rush hour with Boston in my rearview mirror. At least I beat the traffic, so things were already looking up. Now, this all happened in early December just before the holidays, lots of breakups happen around then. I knew I was coming back home anyway. But I figured I'd drive out to Denver, get set up and fly home for the holidays. That was my grand plan, but like Uncle Bruno says, sometimes plans just don't work out the way you want them to."

"Roger that," says Uncle Bruno, spreading pillows on the couch in front of the fireplace.

"I was humming along on the Interstate; I'd been driving for nearly thirty hours straight. It was almost midnight the next day and I was already in Kansas, just outside of Salinas. Kansas is just one flat plane that goes on forever. The weather kept getting worse and worse. A Kansas snowstorm makes this one look mild because the wind gusts out there are brutal with nothing to block them. At least we have trees here. Kansas has no trees, just miles of naked farmland. My visibility was down to about ten-feet as I was driving into this monster blizzard going maybe forty miles an hour. Then I noticed my gas gauge was sitting just on top of E, for empty. That old Lincoln, she never gave me any warning. She'd go from a quarter-tank down to empty in one big gulp. Then it dawned on me, I hadn't seen another car on the highway going in either direction for the last hundred miles.

Just then, right on cue, I spotted an exit with one of those Food-Fuel-Lodging signs. Alleluia. Suddenly I found religion...funny how that happens when all rational hope is lost. I pulled off the highway and right into the gas station, which was all dark and closed. To make matters even worse, it was a Sunday. I was stuck in a blizzard in the middle of nowhere, I mean Kansas, on Sunday. Of course everyone's home all cozy in bed and fast asleep, what else would you expect in Kansas on a Sunday night."

"That's the thing about cell phones, there's never any reception when you need it most."

"Wouldn't have mattered anyway, Gina, I was the last guy on the planet without a cell phone, never liked them. They take you out of the moment. It's like putting everyone else you're talking to and spending time with on hold while you take another call. Horrible invention, but might have come in handy that night."

"Rebel without a cell phone." Uncle Bruno grabs another brownie then passes the plate around to everyone. "They're really good, Samsong. I can't stop eating them."

"Yes, Uncle Bruno, we can see that. So I was beat down from all the drama and knew I was going to have to sleep in the Lincoln and wait for them to open the station in the morning. I grabbed some clothes and my sleeping bag from the trunk then crammed the clothes into the stuff-sack to make a pillow. It was cozy, me all sprawled out on the long back seat with the wind hollering outside. Remember now, I hadn't slept for over thirty hours, so I was dead tired. I figured I'd let the Lincoln run for a little bit to heat up the inside, then turn off the motor and sleep the night away until the station opened in the morning. Then I'd fill her up, jump back on the Interstate and hit Denver by late afternoon, just in time for Happy Hour. That was my plan anyway."

"I never did turn that motor off. Soon as I laid my head down and closed my eyes with the heat turned up full blast, the wind and snow gusting outside made me feel all snuggly inside my sleeping bag, I just fell right to sleep in about ten seconds. When I finally woke up it was already afternoon. I'd slept for thirteen hours, by far the deepest and longest sleep I ever had. I felt great. I couldn't tell if the gas station was open yet because a snow drift had covered up the Lincoln completely. It looked like a big dinosaur egg all covered in snow. My suicide doors on the Lincoln were frozen together so they wouldn't open. Now, there's one good thing that did happen, one tiny miracle in the house of horrors I'd been trapped in those last few days. Cars back then had huge batteries. I still had some juice left, just enough to open a window and climb out, more like, tunnel out of the snowdrift.

It must have been eight feet high. I started digging the Lincoln out with my hands and feet in what felt like thirty-below-zero temperature. But at least it wasn't snowing anymore. To make a long story short..."

"Too late," laughs Uncle Bruno as he uncorks another bottle of vin rouge.

"Okay, to make my long story just a bit longer, I pushed my Lincoln over to the pumps and waited for someone to show up. There was no sign of life anywhere, for miles. But I figured, that's how Kansas is, normally. Then it happens, my second miracle, and this one's a doozy. Right before my very eyes, the pump lit up, the numbers zeroed out and the message read, BEGIN PUMPING. I couldn't believe what I was seeing. I didn't even put a card or anything in, and the pump started working all by itself. I looked around thinking it was one of those Kansas setups, but I didn't even care. All I could feel was the wind chilling through my body down to the bone. I wanted out of there. I filled my tank, with premium, fired up the Lincoln, turned the heat up full blast and I was on the road again, doing eighty down the Interstate with not a cop in sight."

"I thought about leaving some money and a note but then it hit me, why disrespect the miracle? Even if that pump just froze overnight, went crazy and started giving out free gas, I don't want to know about it. To me, in that desperate moment, it was my very own miracle, Emmett's Miracle. Who was I to question why? I took the whole thing as a sign, or a giant kick in the ass, whatever you want to call it. I turned the Lincoln around and forgot all about going to Denver and starting over. I drove straight home to be with my family for the holidays. It was the only year I ever showed up early. So you see, Uncle Bruno, you wanted to escape all that Afghani heat, and I was consumed by a Kansas blizzard but we both made it back to the place we wanted to be the most, home here with you, Samantha."

Sebastian jumps up from the couch. "I've got an idea. Feels like it's high time the Strange Family Band made some music so Mom and Dad have some romping noise to come home to. I'm getting my trumpet, you guys start warming up. Let's show Roma how we still rock the holidays. Let's wake this town up, Strange Family style."

Sebastian is instantly gone. We can hear him upstairs, rummaging through his room, moving things around looking for his trumpet, which I know is underneath his bed, just like always. Uncle Bruno pours us all another glass of vin rouge, then begins warming up his saxophone with "Moon River." Emmett starts playing his Boogie-Woogie Shuffle, the rhythm that never ends if you play it right. I put on my red beret and tune up the fiddle. I never ever play without my red beret anymore. It makes me feel like I'm in Paris playing along the River Seine as romantic couples stroll by on a beautiful spring evening, just like in the movies. Gina grabs her guitar and reminds us she hasn't played since last year.

The thing about the Strange Family Band is that when we get together, we never actually play the same song at the same time. We each play our favorite song, then soften to let one of us take the lead, then we come back together to finish in a wild cacophony of Strange symphonic splendor. It might sound chaotic to the untrained ear, but we have so much fun making our own kind of music, we just don't ever want to stop. Oh, and we always wear hats when we play. That's our one and only Strange Family Band requirement.

We play for hours and hours. Uncle Bruno wearing his cowboy hat, hogs most of the solos blowing his sax, just like every year. Emmet's got on his pith helmet, the one he always wore on our backyard adventures when we were kids; well, I was a kid and he was my big brother who took the time to play with me.

Sebastian is on his trumpet wearing his Daniel Boone coonskin cap with the tail dangling down the back. Gina's wearing her Panama hat, the one she brought back when she went to see the canal. We play until we can't play no more, and then we play just a little bit more. The storm rages outside, like a monster trying to get in, the lights flicker and the fire keeps dancing in rhythm as we play every song we know, and even some we don't. Finally, Uncle Bruno falls back on the pillows and says he surrenders.

"That's it, I'm out of breath. I don't even have any saliva left. I can't feel my lips anymore. That can't be good. SammyKins, go get a fork and stick it in me 'cause I'm all done."

Sebastian blows a soft Taps on his trumpet as we all find our regular spots on the couch.

"God we're good," Gina says as she falls back on the big red oversized pillow, always her favorite. "I think we get better every year. Uncle Bruno, you've got to give up some of those solos. You're hogging them all."

"You have to jump in faster, Gina, otherwise we lose our beat. I was just keeping things going. That's the sax man's job."

Uncle Bruno closes his eyes and in seconds, he's asleep. Emmett and Sebastian are already dozing at the other end of the couch, with Sebastian using Emmett's shoulder as his pillow. Only Gina and myself are still awake, listening to the wind as the fire dies down.

"They'll be here, Samantha. They always come home to their little girl. It's just a bigger storm this year, making it even harder to get through. You'll see, they'll be here soon. I remember just a few years ago how I had such a hard time coming home. First, my flight was postponed. Then, when it finally did take off, we flew into a storm and hit heavy turbulence. Carts were flying down the aisle, overhead compartments dumping everything on our heads. It was horrible. The oxygen masks dropped down and people started praying and calling their families. It was complete chaos for a few minutes and then suddenly, just like that, everything went calm and the plane stopped shaking as the pilot flew us out of the storm and landed us way ahead of schedule."

"We all just sat there with the same dazed look, staring at each other in disbelief at what had just happened, like we had cheated death. It was very late when we finally taxied up and unloaded, so the airport was empty. But I'd never seen an airport so desolate. We couldn't even find anyone to ask where our luggage was. I know I was in shock because I still can't remember anything from when I left the airport that night."

"The next thing I know, I'm standing outside the door in the snow, watching you guys in here and feeling so happy to be home. Don't worry, Samantha, Mom and Dad will get here too. It's where they want to be, where they belong, with the people they love. It's our very own piece of heaven when we're all together. You know what? Watching these guys sleep makes me feel so tired. I'm going to close my eyes for just a little while. You should too, Samantha. You'll need your energy for when they get home. Tell Uncle Bruno to stop snoring so loud..."

Gina pulls her Panama hat down over her eyes and falls into a peaceful sleep. I watch the flames flicker down. The snow has covered the windows, sealing us all in. I throw quilts over my sleeping beauties and pull the comforter over Gina and me. I don't want to sleep but I can't fight it anymore. I feel my eyes closing as I'm pulled deep inside my head. Sleep takes me. Sleep takes us all, one by one...as I drift off I can hear my dad telling me how life is truly about the people you love and the people who love you back. They are your world. It really is that simple, that's all that matters. When we move on from this life the love doesn't stop and the people don't go away. We're always connected. I know, no matter what, we're always going to be the Strange Family, together in our big white house on top of the hill keeping watch over our beautiful little mountain town of Roma...

I open my eyes to the sound of voices. It must be Mom and Dad, everyone else is still asleep. I run into the kitchen and there they are, busy cooking breakfast, or maybe lunch. I don't even know what time it is.

"Hello, Samantha. Come on over here and give your mom and dad a big hug", Mom says, still wearing her coat.

"Sorry we couldn't get home sooner. Oh, Sammy, it's so good to see you. Looks like you guys had quite the party." Dad holds up four empty wine bottles.

"I'm going to have a chat with Uncle Bruno about his wine selection. Maybe next year, don't go so expensive."

35

"I tried to wait up for you but when everyone else fell asleep I just couldn't keep my eyes open." Dad puts on his chef hat and starts pounding pizza dough.

Mom looks over at me and smiles. "Thank you, Samantha, for keeping us all together. You're our shining star, always guiding us back home."

"Love you, Mom and Dad. I'll go wake them up. It's going to be our best holidays ever."

I know a few things...I know I'll be eighteen in a few years, old enough to be on my own and move back into our home again, where I belong. My family is here. They always will be. My happy memories are here too, my only happy memories. The other night, just before I came up to the house to get things ready, I was playing my fiddle outside the town meeting. I watched everyone walk by, saw the sadness in their eyes and heard their whispers as they dropped money in my case. 'Poor kid'... 'Her whole family gone'... 'Always talking to herself'... 'Staying with the Harrisons until she's old enough to be on her own'... 'All alone on the holidays'...Funny how only Little Ivan winked at me, gave me a one-hundred-dollar bill and said, "Tell them all I say hello, Sammy-Do." Ivan understands things.

Well I'm just fine, I couldn't be happier. I'm with the people I love and everybody's home now. Christmas is the only time of year when I get to see them like I remember them, the way we were.

These things I do know for sure—Uncle Bruno, he never did make it back from that ambush in Afghanistan. I know Emmett fell asleep in his Lincoln in that Kansas blizzard and never woke up. I know Sebastian's dormitory fire killed his entire freshman class, including him. I know Gina's plane crashed into the Atlantic ocean just after takeoff and there were no survivors.

Just three years ago on this very night, I know my mom and dad died in that car accident on the highway, the one that shut down both lanes so nobody could get home for Christmas Eve. But I know this even more...I know they are all still here with me, watching over me, because we are the Strange family always and forever.

And I know that better than ever today.

Happy Holidays Roma.

# DIGGER PATROL

"HOLY SHIT...I can't even believe we made it. They were all over us. Get this fuckin chopper airborne now. Is anybody listening to me? Let's go. Luther, get that flyboy moving. Put a gun to his head if you need to, just get us the hell out of here. BOOM, BLAST, PETUUM, RAT-ATATATAT, ZING..."

"What the hell just happened back there, Luther? It's like they were waiting for us. Secure area my ass."

"We got some bad Intel on this one, that's for sure. That's all the bodies we're pulling out for now. We better be gone."

"Yeah Luth, bad Intel that's it...for the third time this month. I say someone at HQ has it in for us. Who cares, right? We're just the fuckup brigade, the Digger Patrol."

"He's bleeding pretty bad from his chest and neck. I don't think he's gonna make it. Radio ahead, tell them to have medical evac ready."

"Look at Luther. He's bleeding from both ears and doesn't even know it. Hold on Luth, we'll get you cleaned up."

"Well there's nothing we can do for him now. Stick in two more hits of morphine and maybe the docs can save his ass back at base. One way or another, he's punched his ticket out of this wasteland."

"We're flying low now, but at least we're up, up and away. The higher we get, the colder I feel. Must be that Afghan mountain air. I can hear the bullets and see the shoulder rockets screaming by, just barely missing us.

Suddenly, it's nighttime. I can see a beautiful full moon. What time is it? Why is it so dark?"

BOOM. CLINK, CLANK, CLANK, CLANK..."one of those ground to air missiles gets lucky and hits our back rotor. Sounds like the blade's messed up, but we still have enough power to stay airborne, barely. Just get us home, right, Luth? What are we about fifty klicks out? We should be touching down at base in about twenty minutes."

"Regis, how many did we pull?"

"Luther always checks with Regis before he calls in to HQ with the tally. Going out they tell us how many are MIA. Coming in we tell them how many bodies we retrieved. Regis is always the counter. He records the dog tags and gives the names to Luther who radios in to make it official, just in case we don't make it back."

"Three, Luther. Our mission was five. Danko and Gaines are still out there somewhere. Jackson saw something on the hill, but he ran into that bee's nest. All the ways there are to die out here and Jackson finds an actual bee's nest. Did you see him jumping around trying not to get stung? How about Sergeant Bruno leading the charge like he did? What got into him? Never saw anything like it. I thought we were all goners, then Bruno takes off, up and over that hill like a mountain Billy goat. He ran fast for a big man. I just ducked behind him and followed his line all the way to the chopper. I could barely keep up with him, and he was carrying a body. Never saw anything like it."

Jackson's sitting in the back of the chopper, sucking in air like it's his last few breaths before going underwater. He's freaking out. Somebody get Jackson a paper bag. He sounds like he's trying to time his breath to the whoosh of our broken tail blade. I look out the open door. It's even darker now, no more full-moon. Where did the moon go? Will somebody please tell me what time it is? The gunfire and artillery blasts are all gone now. It's a clear, tranquil night. The stars look close enough to touch. I reach out for one, but my bloody hand falls right through, turning it into a faded red star. How can such a dirty war-torn desert transform into this peaceful starlit dreamscape only a few minutes away from our bloody battlefield? Why is Jackson crying?

I look at the battered faces of my Digger Patrol and see four more casualties of an endless war gone out of control– Luther, Jackson, Carbone and Regis–two soul brothers from Harlem, a Wop, one Mexican and me, their Sergeant. We've been together for just over a year now, assigned to the worst detail in AfghanHell. We're the lunatics they send in to collect the bodies after the battle has already been fought and nobody won, because there never was anything to win in the first place.

No one ever really gets assigned to Digger Patrol. It's more like a sentence. Carbone's been here the longest. He slugged his captain and a chaplain all in the same day, actually in the same hour. Sure, Carbone's wound a little tight but he's the kind of guy you want watching your back in a gunfight. The guy never stops shooting. Look at him slouched over there staring right through me. He could be sitting in a bar at Happy Hour somewhere wondering what drink to order with that same empty gaze. Yo Carbone, just another day in paradise, huh.

"Chopper Five to base. We are ten klicks out with our rotor tail hit. We're coming in hard. Repeat...Chopper Five with Digger Patrol coming in hard landing with wounded on board. ETA four minutes. Chopper Five out."

"Hey Luther, switch places with me, I don't have any straps here."

"That's your problem, Regis. Find something heavy to hold on to. Don't let go until we hit the ground and stop moving. Grab a hold of Sergeant Bruno, he's not going anywhere."

Regis pulls off his belt and straps it through the chopper's door frame. He wraps the belt twice around his forearm and tests it for strength, pulling his big self up and down. Yeah, that ought to hold so long as we don't roll over. Regis is big, over six feet, almost as big as Luther. They look like a couple of pulling guards when they get going, big bad linemen looking to mow down anyone who gets in their way. Jackson and Carbone are smaller and faster. We usually fall in behind Regis and Luther using their girth to shield us while we try to locate and collect the soldiers who got left behind. Their job is to kill anything that moves while we grab the bodies. It's a pretty good system. We cover each other's ass and we're usually in and out like a bank job. From the time the chopper hits the ground, we can take care of business in less than ten minutes, unless of course we get pinned down, like today. Then it can take a bit longer, even a lot longer.

Regis is always saying, "Gotta Go, Gotta Go, Gotta Go", like he thinks we're taking too long and the cops are coming. One time he even said, "Forget the cash draw, we gotta go now." We all just looked at each other and started laughing. Regis is from east L.A.– he has a few gang tattoos, so he's paranoid of getting caught by nature; a store robbery or two wouldn't be so far-fetched. It's been six months now since Regis joined our crew. He got caught buying ten kilos of Afghani hashish from some of the local gangsters in Kabul. Our commanding officer gave Regis a choice. He could do ten years in Leavenworth, back home, or serve out two years on Digger Patrol. Right now, I bet he's thinking he should have gone for Leavenworth behind door number one. He would have been much safer today.

Damn, it feels even colder now, can't wait 'til we get back to base. I keep thinking about my mother, how she would always have hot cocoa waiting for me on those cold Vermont winter days when I'd come home from school back in Roma. What a time to think about Mom. I really miss her. Wish she was here right now. I'm so fucking cold.

Luther throws me a look like he can hear what I'm thinking. He lights up that joint he's been holding and passes it to Jackson. I guess he figures if we're going out tonight, we might as well leave on a high note. We're not ever supposed to be smoking on a chopper, especially one shot up as bad as this. Hell, what are they going to do to us? We might as well get high before we touch down. Hey Jackson, pass me that joint.

Jackson, Luther and me, we all came to Digger Patrol together, sort of a package deal. I guess those guys blame me for getting us sent here. After all, I am their sergeant and I do feel a little guilty. But we were all there that night and they did egg me on. Hard to believe it was only a year ago…fucking asshole Bactrian Camel.

It was 0300, that's three in the morning, and everyone was asleep, even the bad guys. I still remember everything so clearly. It was like this war had taken the night off. There was a cool breeze blowing down from the mountains. Luther,

Jackson and me, we were all fucked up, higher than a U-2 spy plane after toking some of the sweetish hashish I'd ever tasted. Jackson had scored it when he was on leave in Jalalabad. We didn't even mind being on guard duty. We could smoke all night, shoot the shit and sleep most of the next day. It really wasn't such a bad deal. There was Luther kicking back, half asleep, talking about some girl he knew in high school who could put both of her legs behind her head; popular girl, she wasn't even a gymnast, just naturally flexible. Jackson was reloading the pipe for another hit. I was sitting up front, playing with the grenade launcher trying to find something to blow up, not really blow up, just make believe. I swear to God I wasn't actually going to shoot it, I was just aiming at stuff...until I spotted that arrogant two-humped camel.

He was standing on top of a boulder, staring right at me like he had night tunnel vision and could see us from four hundred yards away. We were hidden behind some rocks, but I swear, looking through that scope I could see this arrogant camel eye-balling me, just daring me to pull the trigger. I say to Luther, how about I blow this humpback away. Luther leans up, looks at the camel and says that I don't have the balls. Jackson chimes in that I couldn't make the shot anyway because he's too far away and my aim sucks even on a clear day.

Now that's practically a direct challenge if you ask me. Jackson passes me the pipe. I take the mother of all hits and hold it in as I sight the grenade launcher on that big lumpy camel, who's still eyeballing me. Now he's even sneering at me. As I slowly blow out the hashish, my finger lightly squeezes the trigger and launches the grenade.

KABOOM. A direct hit blowing both of those humps right off that uppetty camel's back. Then all hell breaks loose. Jackson and Luther jump up and start shooting their rifles at where that camel used to be. The whole company wakes up and everyone starts shooting. This goes on for five minutes before they finally figure out that nobody is shooting back. That's when they come looking for us. What they found was three fucked-up marines, one well-used water pipe and enough hashish to feed a family of three for a month. Even worse, we hadn't had time to get our stories straight, so we were forced to tell the truth. Did you know the Bactrian camel is a revered animal in Afghanistan? It's like the sacred cow in India, only with two humps. It's a highly valued animal. I didn't know about that then, but I know everything there is to know about the Bactrian camel now.

I guess I can understand why the guys are still a little sore at me. I mean, I am their Sergeant. I should have known better. I'm the guy who's supposed to keep them out of trouble. But shit, that's no reason not to share the joint with me now. That camel is water under the bridge, far as I'm concerned. He's in a better place now, camel heaven. What's done is done. Now let's land this chopper and go get some beers and grub. I'm starved, and oh so thirsty.

"OK, boys. Hold on to something that don't move. This is gonna be a rough one. See you guys at the bar. Sergeant Bruno's buying."

Luther's got some balls joking at a time like this. I never buy. Nobody does. I look over at Regis who tests his strap one more time for good luck. He pulls down hard with his entire body weight, probably two hundred and fifty pounds. The belt rips the frame from its hinges, leaving Regis attached to nothing and holding the door frame in his hands. Regis looks at me like he's just seen a ghost. We're about to hit. He grabs on to me like I'm a life preserver as the chopper crashes down, rolling us over and over. CRASH, BANG, THUD, THUD, CREAK, SCREECH...then silence and lots of flashing lights."

That wasn't so bad. Luther, Jackson and Carbone end up on top of me and Regis, like one of those pileups in a football game. I hear sirens and feel hands everywhere pulling us from the chopper, which is on fire. The pilot is dead, we're gonna need another body-bag, boys. They've got the bags already laid out. They always do when Digger Patrol comes home. I watch them stuff the bags with the three we found, plus the dead pilot. What the fuck? Get your hands off me. What are you guys doing? Don't put me in that bag. Holy shit they're zipping it up. They think I'm dead. Wait a minute, I'm dead? I'm fucking dead? I don't feel cold anymore. I don't feel anything. I smell cocoa. I want to go home to Roma. I want to see Samantha…

# INTO THE MEANWHILE

"Is it in yet?"

"Yes, it is...at least I think so."

"Sounds like a bad date, Ollie. Are you sure? I can't feel anything."

"Yes, there it's in. In this case, it's good you can't feel anything. That wasn't so hard, I mean terrible. To my recollection, we never did have a bad date Cassie. Now just sit back and enjoy that beautiful sunset. Autumn sunsets always were your favorites."

Ollie pulls me closer and puts his strong arm around my frail body. "Don't worry, Cass, they'll be fine. We took care of everything. It was good to see them, nothing like a family barbecue to bring everyone together."

"It was memorable Ollie, I'll give you that." I take a long sip of Margarita and pass the glass to him.

"This is living, just lounging on the porch with my best girl by my side. Does it get any better than this?"

"Best girl. Don't you mean only girl, Oliver Osborne?"

"I do, I do...how do you feel now, Cassie?"

"A little tired, that's all. Maybe a little light headed too. But lately, that's what I call normal."

We take another sip of our Margarita as the red, orange, yellow and blue leaves paint the horizon for a slow setting sun.

## ONE YEAR EARLIER...

"I'm afraid it's bad news, Cassie. The lymphoma has spread."

"But I thought we caught it early, Doctor. You said we caught it very early."

"We did, but lymphatic cancer can be very aggressive. If we fight back just as aggressively with radiation and chemotherapy, we could see positive results, adding years."

"What kind of success rate have you seen with other people at this same stage? Like they say in the movies, give it to me straight, Doc."

"Honestly, Cassie, it's pretty low with stage four. But the chemo usually does buy some time."

"I've seen first-hand what chemotherapy does to people, Doctor Carson. My mother went through chemo. She was vomiting all the time, couldn't hold down any food and she lost all her hair. She never did get it back. Ollie and I have already talked about this. If I don't go the chemo and radiation route, how long do you think I would have before the cancer takes me?"

"At this stage, I'd say anywhere from one to three years. It's hard to predict Cassie. We'll have to monitor how aggressively it spreads from here. There will be increasing pain and fatigue which we can manage with medication for the most part. But eventually you will need constant care. It will be too much for Ollie to handle by himself. What about your kids, are they able to help out?"

"Our girls are so busy with their own lives, Doctor. Lena's a big wig at a bank in Boston, and she has two daughters of her own. As you know, Sophie's an ER nurse here at the county hospital. We hardly ever see Lena, but Sophie comes by every weekend. Ollie and I would prefer not to tell them until we absolutely have to. When do you think that would be Doctor? How soon do things start becoming obvious?"

"I'd say within the next six to twelve months your body will be impacted by weakness and increasing fatigue. It really depends on the individual how fast things happen."

"As Cassie said, Doctor Carson, we've already talked about this possibility."

"What Ollie means, Doctor, is that I really don't want to do the chemo. We want to enjoy each other as is, for as long as we can. Hold the chemo Doctor, just give me that medical marijuana..."

### ONE YEAR LATER...

"To think it's been a year since Doctor Carson gave us the news. He was pretty much right on target with his predictions. I was just fine for most of the year. It's only in the last month or two that I'm feeling it, the throbbing pain Ollie, constantly, all day long. It never goes away, gets even worse at night time."

"You've done great Cassie. Sophie's noticed the changes, but hell, she's a nurse. I'd be worried if she didn't. Lena just thinks you're tired because you're old, because we're both old."

"Why don't you light up some of that medical weed Doctor Carson prescribed. I have to admit, Ollie, it really has helped."

"I told you it would. It's helped me too Cassie. I'm sleeping like a baby again. Here, take a good puff and hold it in as long as you can. Just a couple of puffs of this and we'll both be sleeping soundly within the hour."

"Hold me tight, Ollie. I want to feel your hand holding mine when I drop off. Don't let go. Never let me go."

"Do you remember the first time we held hands, Cassie"?

"Sure I do, the very last day of the eighth grade when those boys were being mean to me on my walk home from school. You were my hero Ollie, showing up to save the day like you did."

"Yes, Cassie, something I should probably tell you about that day. I guess now is as good a time as any. You see, that whole thing was my fault. I saw you walking home from school all year long and got the big idea to start walking home too, instead of taking the bus. I thought maybe we could start walking home together. Come springtime, about a month before the end of school, I stopped taking the bus and started walking a respectable distance behind you."

"I remember seeing you, Ollie. I couldn't understand why you were walking so slow. I stopped and took rests but you still never caught up to me."

"See, that was my diabolical plan Cassie. I started off walking way behind you, then each day caught up just a little bit closer, so I wouldn't scare you off."

"Why didn't you just walk home with me, Ollie? That would have been fine by me."

"Oh, sure it makes sense now. But not in the mind of an awkward eighth grade boy who had a big crush on that beautiful blue-eyed girl sitting in the fourth row he couldn't even talk to. No, Cassie, everything had to be just right. That last day of school, I was ready."

"The last day of the eighth grade was horrible for me! My parents thought I might need therapy to get over it. They almost put me in a boarding school, with nuns. What do you mean, it was your fault?"

"Things just got out of hand. Do you remember who the boys were who chased you home?"

"I've never been able to forget them. It was the Murphy brothers, all three of them. I could never tell them apart. That Perkins kid was there, and that other kid who got left back, Hagen. They were all there."

"Well, Cass, those were the kids I rode the bus home with until I decided not to, just so I could follow you home. I guess they were a little mad at me for quitting the bus. They felt like I ditched them for you, which I did."

"Oh Ollie, you say the sweetest things, seventy years later. But why did they start chasing me? I fell on the hill and skinned both my knees."

"I know, I saw you, but that was when everything went crazy. Now remember, this was the special day I had been planning for all that Spring. I was going to carry your books and buy you an ice cream cone. I had the money and everything. I started walking behind you like always, and just as I was catching up I turned around and saw those guys running to catch up to me. I started walking faster, and then began jogging, thinking if they saw me with you they might back off and go away. But instead, I tripped and fell just before the hill. They ran past me like we were in a race. You turned around, saw them coming and took off like a deer running up that hill. All I could think was, this is horrible, this is just terrible, Cassie's never going to like me now."

"I can still remember their faces, all red, sweaty and angry, like a lynch mob. I almost climbed a tree. I thought they were going to kill me and I didn't even know why."

"Yeah, they thought it was a game. I was trying to catch up to them, so they ran even faster. They thought you were racing them, so they ran after you, kind of like a fox hunt. For a bunch of chubby kids, they ran fast that day. But so did you Cassie. I was really impressed with your speed."

"Thanks, Ollie. I'm always faster when I'm running for my life. But wait a minute, why did they start throwing rocks at my house?"

"Yes, I thought that was a bit odd also. I asked the Murphy brothers about that when I was yelling at them. They said they were heaving the rocks over your roof just to see if they could. But Pauly Perkins had a weak arm and kept hitting your house. He never could throw. He was horrible at kickball too."

"I finally made it to my house, ran inside and locked the door. All I could see from looking out our front window was those mean boys hiding behind the bushes throwing huge rocks from the road. Then, out of nowhere comes my hero Oliver Osborne running up the hill, huffing and puffing but still my knight in shining armor. Or so I thought until today."

"No, I was. I mean, I am, Cassie. I was just very disappointed with how things worked out that afternoon, which was supposed to be our big day. Instead, it became the girl of my dreams running for her life away from my friends. All I saw was you looking out your front window seeing me with that crazy mob that chased you home. That wasn't how I planned it at all."

"What was it you said to make them all go away, Ollie? I do remember how suddenly they were gone from in front of my house, running down the street like they were late for dinner."

"I made them an offer they couldn't refuse. It was the only way I could think of to get rid of them in a hurry. Remember when I said I'd saved up my money to buy you and me ice cream cones. Well, Cassie, you never did get that ice cream cone because I gave my ten dollars to those guys just to make them disappear. They went running down the street alright, straight to the ice cream parlor. It only looked like I scared them away. Really, I just paid them off."

"My hero Ollie, that handsome boy who lived up the block...but you did knock on my door to see if I was alright. Tell me at least that part's true. We did go for a walk that day. You even held my hand, a pretty big deal for an eighth grader who never even talked to a girl before."

"Yes, Cassie, that part's all true and I've been holding your hand ever since that horrific day, which actually turned out to be our beautiful beginning. I seem to remember a kiss at the end of that walk."

"I remember it too, Ollie. Only I remember me kissing you, and you just standing there frozen like a statue for five minutes after I went inside my house. I watched you from my bedroom window upstairs, just standing still with that big goofy grin until finally you took off and ran all the way home. I even saw that funny little dance you did on your front lawn."

"You saw that did you; funny how the truth finally comes out. That was my touchdown dance. I believe the kids today call it a 'twurk'. I invented it. Always did it when I was very happy, or whenever I scored a touchdown-which was a lot in grade school.

"Well, I guess you're still my hero, Ollie. Best and worst last day of school, first day of summer ever. The most exciting too. How about the first time we laid eyes on each other? Do you remember that?"

"It had to be the first grade, no kindergarten, the very first day of school. I remember it well. I think you threw me off the monkey bars. You said they were your monkey-bars and I had to be invited to climb on them."

"I do remember being strangely possessive of those monkey bars. But that wasn't the first time we met. Ah-hah, you forgot, Ollie Osborne. Let me just shift my arm a bit. It's falling asleep before the rest of me. But don't let go of my hand, Ollie, you promised to never let go."

"I know Cass, I got you. Hand-in-hand, now and forever. I'll just squeeze a little tighter. Is that better, can you feel me now?"

"Yes, that's much better. First time we met was outside Eideltyme Deli, that place that made those great sandwiches. We were just born, maybe six months old, plus two weeks because I am older than you..."

"My Mrs. Robinson."

"You and your mom were going inside just as me and my mom were coming out of the deli. My mom said it was a very cold and windy February afternoon. They hadn't met yet, but because they were each carrying newborn babies they got into a long conversation. Mom said we just stared at each other the whole time they were talking, which was a good twenty minutes. They were laughing about how we couldn't take our eyes off each other. We even started cooing back and forth, like baby flirting. Our Moms became friends that freezing February day, while you and I made our first connection. That was the first time we met, Ollie. I can't believe you don't remember that."

"I really don't really remember much from six months old, something about the brain not being formed yet. Clearly, your mom filled you in on our family histories much better than mine did. I do remember Eideltyme though with those big deli sandwiches. They just don't make delis like that anymore. How about this–I remember taking swimming lessons at the YMCA pool together. I recall you didn't want to go underwater, so they blew in your face and dunked you under."

"That's what they do to all the babies to help them go underwater."

"Yes, Cassie, they do. But we were five. You were the only kid in our class who refused to put her face in the water. You even invented your own stroke; it was a cross between a breast and a side stroke, with your head held high the entire time and your hair never getting wet. It always made me laugh watching you do laps like that."

"Again, it was our moms who decided we should do swimming lessons together. I dreaded those classes with you always jumping off the side of the pool just to splash me. By the way, my stroke you found so hilarious is called the New Zealand Elementary Sidestroke. It's a real thing."

"To this day, I've never seen anyone else swim like that. But I always loved watching you do it, my very own

Esther Williams. New Zealand huh, the land where they don't like to get their hair wet."

"Make fun if you want, Ollie, but I'm pretty sure it's an Olympic event. Wow, I can really feel it now. I'm so drowsy. Don't think I can stay awake too much longer. How about you, Ollie? Are you feeling sleepy yet?"

"I've been feeling sleepy for the last few years, Cassie. I just always wait for you to drift off first, in case you need something."

"I so love looking down the mountain at the nighttime lights of Roma. Look, there are lights on again at the Strange house. I thought nobody was living there since the accident. They were such lovely neighbors. What is the little girl's name?"

"Samantha, I see her around town playing her fiddle. She's very good. I think they left the house to her, so when she's old enough she can move back in. Right now, she's staying with one of the families in town, the Harrison's I believe. Maybe she's visiting tonight. After all, it is her home."

"We were here in Roma for the glory years, Ollie. It was a great place to raise our kids, such a pretty town. But so much has changed. Roma's just not what she used to be. I'm so glad our girls moved away. I've noticed things don't end well for the kids who stick around here. Remember our family trips? What trip was your favorite one, Ollie?"

"I loved them all, Cass. But you know in my mind Iceland always stands out as our most adventurous–eating fish for breakfast; twenty-four-hour sunlight; hiking above and then behind those waterfalls–amazing; and those Icelandic ponies prancing around like unicorns, magical. Remember when I put Sophie on that stallion?"

"I warned you not to..."

"I know, but she felt left out. She wanted to ride a real horse all by herself, not just get led around the pony ring like a little kid."

"She was seven, Ollie. She was a little kid."

"In retrospect, I do see your point. I probably should have chosen a different horse instead of that stallion named Thunder. But he was the horse she wanted to ride. Who knew he was going to take off on a gallop like that? I was so proud of Soph, the way she hung on for dear life to his mane until he came to that abrupt stop just before the fence. I remember that big grin on her face when she jumped off into my arms. You know what she said?"

"Yes, I seem to remember the exact words from over the years...Oh, Daddy, I want to do that again. You both love telling me that story, even though I stood right there watching, in horror."

"Makes for a great memory though. How about you, Cass? Favorite trip?"

"Oh, you know mine Ollie, Hawaii. I'd always wanted to go there, and we finally did. Hawaii, especially Maui, lived up to all my dreams. The flowers, the beaches, the dolphins, the whales, and all those luaus we went to–just so wonderful. Also, that rock you insisted on jumping off with Sophie...not so wonderful."

"For the final record, that was her idea. I do admit, as we were climbing up I knew we'd never be able to climb back down. It was way too slippery, and the waves were crashing in... the only safe way down was to jump. I remember holding her little head to my chest and off we went from thirty feet up. There were grown men and women chickening out up there, and here's this little kid making the jump. Soon as we hit the water, I pushed her up to the surface as I plunged to the bottom watching her swim like a little tadpole. When I came back up, Sophie's first words to me were, "Daddy, I never want to do that again."

"Could you hear the people on the beach screaming, look at that crazy guy, he's jumping off Black Rock with his little kid?"

"No, I couldn't hear them. What I did hear when we made the jump was all those same people cheering. Funny how that happens, going from villain to hero in one unforgettable leap."

"I do remember the cheering. Now Sophie always says she wants to go back to Maui, to Black Rock, and jump off again. Go figure...it's been a beautiful journey, Ollie. Thank you for everything."

"Back at you, Cass. I wouldn't change a thing, except for that last day of eighth grade. That could have gone a whole lot better."

"I really feel it now, Ollie. I'm drifting off. Hold me tighter. How about you? Ready?"

"I'm right here with you, Cassie, just like always. Let's fall asleep together. I'll see you 'into the meanwhile', like our girls used to say. Remember when it was naptime and they wanted us to all go to sleep together so we could meet up on the other side? Sophie called it, "going into the meanwhile." I always liked that. Love you Cass, always have and always will. I'm ready too. Don't the stars seem so close tonight? Cass, you there? Alright girl, I'm right behind you...time to find out what's next."

## Mid-Morning Next Day...

...'I knew Sophie would come. She always comes to visit around this time every Sunday, just to check up on us'.

"Yes, Doctor Carson, I called you first, as you asked. I dropped by this morning and found them outside on the porch. The morphine drips are still in their arms. Yes, I already checked, they're gone, still holding hands and I swear they're smiling. No, I won't touch anything. I'll stay right here with them. They look so peaceful and happy. Thanks again, Doctor Carson, for helping them. I'll see you soon."

"I'm happy for you, Mom and Dad. Cassie and Ollie Osborne, always together in life, so why not in death. Hand in hand, even. Nice touch."

'We'll always be right here with you, Sophie, watching over our beautiful girls and dreamy grandchildren. Now, look on the table under the Margarita glass. Go ahead it's right there'.

"What's this? Of course you left a note. I knew you'd never leave me and Lena without having the last word..."

***No Regrets***
*We laughed, We cried,*
*We hoped for the best, We gave our dreams a good try;*
*We held each other close when times were so tough,*
*We found ways to laugh through days all too rough;*
*We traveled the world, We hiked the great peaks,*
*We explored far away, We surfed secret beach;*
*We danced around bonfires and caught shooting stars,*
*Then walked hand in hand toward light from afar;*
*Now it's our time to move on together,*
*We have no regrets, Life here with you could not have been better —*
*Bientot Kids…Love and Beyond, Your Mom & Dad,*

*Cass & Ollie*

'Oh the stars, Ollie, I always knew it was all about the stars. It had to be. More stars than people who have ever lived. So many lights to explore. It's just the beginning of our journey, Ollie, not the end. I knew it,  I just always knew it'.

'And we get to do it together, Cassie. Together forever with my sweetheart, my Cassie. Now slow down, I'm still running to catch up with you'…

## BATTLE OF THE HIGH HOLIES

Something's going on up there. You can see it if you sit here long enough and pay close attention. I can't believe I'm the only one who has taken notice. I don't even have a telescope…

The stars are fighting with each other. They're coming closer and closer. That's why we're seeing all these fires up in the hills around Roma. It's not us kids starting them like everyone thinks. It's what's left of those dead stars falling from the night sky. A few almost hit me. But I just stay in my spot underneath Overlook Rock and so far so good, no direct hits, just the best star-show anyone has ever seen. I probably should tell somebody about what I'm seeing. But isn't it their job to notice stuff like this? Maybe it's only happening up above Roma where everyone seems too busy and worried to look up at the stars anymore. They should, though, before it's too damn late.

I started coming up here about two years ago to get away from people, maybe smoke a joint or two, and do some thinking about how to get the hell out of Roma.

Fall and winter are my favorite seasons to hike because the skies are so dark, making the stars seem even closer. I'd only been coming up here a couple of weeks when I noticed what looked like three shooting stars coming out of the Big Dipper. Now I'm no Galileo, but I do know my way around the stars just from our class trips to the planetarium and reading a bunch of astronomy books. I always use the Big Dipper to find the Little Dipper, which takes me right to Polaris, the North Star, shining bright and beautiful inside

Little Ursa the baby bear, my personal favorite. But I swear that first night, I'm laying back on a big boulder, taking a couple of tokes, when suddenly I see three shooting stars coming out of the Big Dipper aiming straight for Polaris. They were moving supersonic fast in a triangle formation, like fighter jets do. Just when they were getting close to Polaris— looked about three feet away from my view, which probably equals a few million miles in outer space—just as they were getting within spitting distance, Polaris shot out three beams of light–a red, a blue and a green exploding the three shooting stars. I thought it might have been the weed that made me hallucinate the whole thing, but don't you know just five minutes later three flaming rocks came falling out of the sky and landed just a hundred feet from where I'm sitting right now. What did I do? What do you think I did? I screamed like a little girl who just saw her first snake and ran fast as this fat boy can run, all the way down the mountain road back to Roma. That's what I did. Passed that kid, Samantha, playing her fiddle along the road on the way down. She was wearing a red beret and talking to herself as she played, "Singin' in the Rain." Strange little girl that Samantha, kind of spooky, if you ask me.

I'm like a bear in the winter, I like to hibernate. A few years ago, I found this old stone hut built way back in the 1930s during the Depression years so that hikers and mountain climbers had a place to stay overnight. It's tucked away, right underneath Overlook Rock, looking down on Roma and the whole valley. From November through March, I set up camp here watching the stars, smoking my weed, reading my books and sleeping the winter months away. The hut has a wood burning stove and some old bunk beds, so it gets cozy at night with the wind howling through the mountain notch and the snow blowing wild outside. My parents figure I'm sleeping over somebody's house when I'm not home. They're usually too busy working or drinking to even notice I'm gone. I come up here with my charts and my astronomy books to explore the universe, and try to figure out what the hell is going on with our star system. I shower at the school gym and steal whatever food I can from the general store. Usually I just take some bread and peanut butter, a little honey and beef jerky. I think Rufus, the store's owner, knows I'm taking stuff but he never says anything because he probably feels sorry for me. I can always tell when people feel sorry for me; I'd rather they hate me than feel sorry for me.

Don't kid yourself, bears have it made in the winter. All we do is stay at home in our cozy dark den and sleep peacefully. Everyone thinks bears sleep straight through the winter but that's not true. We wake up in the middle of our long night just like regular people do. But the difference is, bears don't stay awake. We just stretch a little bit, listen to the wind, see if it's still snowing, take a piss and fall back into a deep sleep for a few more weeks. If people could get back to sleep as easily as bears do they would probably be a whole lot happier, instead of walking around miserable all the time. Turns out only bears seem to know the key to happiness...it's sleep, lots of it and for long periods of time. People should hibernate too. They'd be a lot easier to get along with.

If you look up there at the Little Dipper's ladle you can see it feeds into Ursa Minor, the she-bear cub. The Little Dipper forms the butt of little Ursa which is my favorite constellation because you can actually make out the bear outline so clearly. She looks like a bear. Sometimes I spend the whole night trying to make out the figures my charts say are up there and I just cannot find them. Baby Ursa is easy though. Just go to the top of the Little Dipper and follow it all the way down to the curve that is Ursa's tush, and you have arrived.

Way back when, it was Ptolemy who was the first guy to notice the Big and Little Ursas. That was in the second century B.C. and he didn't have a telescope either. I guess he got fed up with everyone too, so he started sleeping outside and looking up at the stars for answers. It's way more peaceful.

Ptolemy got to name Ursa. He made her one of the forty-eight original constellations. Now all these years later, I get to watch her brightest star Polaris fight back against the Big and Little Dippers in a cage match to the end. Those Greeks, they really knew how to party with the stars.

Everybody knows the Big Dipper and the Little Dipper are both made up of seven stars each. Polaris, aka the North Star and the brightest star in our sky on most nights, sits just below the Big Dipper at the tail end of the Little Dipper. Together, they rule the night sky for as far as you can see, and much further beyond that. When you look up, the first thing you always notice is the Big Dipper. Then your eye just naturally moves to the Little Dipper, and then on over to Polaris. It's like they're sitting next to each other in a VIP box. You can't help noticing them. You have to pay respect to these big three before you can look anywhere else.

I have a theory, a big one I believe. It's come to me after many long nights and many deep tokes spent watching these three super star-powers shimmering high up above, and now lately seeing them shoot rocket beams and laser lights at each other. What if, just what if, Big, Little and Polaris are really God, Jesus and Holy Ghost, that all-knowing we have all the answers Trinity we've been wondering about and praying to for miracles all these thousands of years? And what if, just what if, they're pissed off at each other for something that happened recently, and that's why they're throwing fireballs back and forth at each other that end up landing down here around Roma? I know you're probably thinking that's just the weed talking, but I'm telling you, something's going on up there.

Something big, something angry is happening, like God, Jesus and the Holy Ghost are throwing down, and not one of them is backing off. It's no different than what goes on down here every day in Roma, and most other places too. First, you've got your Jesus Freaks–the Born-Agains, those Evangelicals and some Catholics too–all running around telling people how their faith is the best and if everyone doesn't get on board with Jesus, and only Jesus, they're going to live a horrible life, and then go straight to hell. That's fireball number one, low and inside from the Little Dipper.

Fireball number two comes up and away from the Big Dipper representing the Jewish people, who say they are the chosen ones, and only they have a direct line to God, everyone else is pretty much shtupped. Very old-school the Jewish, by-passing both Jesus and the Holy Ghost, going directly to the CEO. No Holy Trinity for them, just the almighty creator of everything and everyone, all by himself, and themselves. I call them the God Almighties.

Last, certainly not the least in Roma and this country we all live in, are the Holy Ghosts. Fireball number three comes in fast and furious, right down the middle from Polaris, representing the old school Protestants. I was born and raised one in the Presbyterian church. Sure, we may grab for Jesus at the very end, pay a little lip service to God on the holidays, but our real allegiance is to the Chief Operating Officer, the one in charge of making good things happen in the here and now on Planet Earth, our very own Holy Ghost. So just think, what if these big three are fighting up there like we're fighting down here? Not good at all, and probably doesn't end well for anyone. Just saying, it's my theory. But what if?

It's not so far-fetched if you think about it, sit back, and watch the night skies long enough. They're lobbing proton torpedoes at each other and the shrapnel is landing down here. The fragments are getting bigger and hotter, just like the fires that get blamed on me and my boys. I do find it hard to believe that these hills outside Roma are the only place on Planet Earth this star show is happening, though Roma has always considered itself a special place, so much better than the towns and villages that surround us. Years ago, that was true. Today though, the Roma I know has fallen to maybe even a cut below these other shabby towns, and things are getting worse by the day.

But what do I know? I'm just a dumb kid who hardly ever goes to school anymore. I mean, what's the point? They're talking about closing Roma's school next year anyway and busing us all the way to Etrusca, or Babylon even. That's a thirty-minute ride, every day. No, my thinking is all about how to get the hell out of Roma and finish school somewhere else, far away from here. I've got an aunt in Colorado, but I don't think she likes me. I have an uncle who lives up in Canada; Calgary I believe, but I know for a fact he doesn't like me. I think because they don't like my mom and dad they just carry their dislike over to me. Outside of maybe making a few colorful remarks at family parties, I can't remember ever doing anything bad or mean to them. I did spill some red wine on my Aunt Peggy's new dress once; I did mention to my Uncle Jack that he was getting fatter every time I saw him. But these are little things that go on in every family; no reason to turn their backs on a kid, a relative, who needs a safe place to finish school before the end of the world. Isn't that what family is for?

I think I know what the High Holies are pissed off about. It's all these different religions, each claiming their god, their faith, their belief system is better than the rest. To me, religions are like fast food chains—McDonalds, Burger King, Wendy's, Taco Bell, Kentucky Fried Chicken...there's one on every corner and they're all saying their fast food is better than the other guy's. But in the end, it's all just good-tasting grease. In my mind, there either is or isn't a God, one big kahuna with all the answers. If there is, great, he or she sure has a lot of explaining to do. If there isn't any God, then that means this is it, just one big sloppy accident called life on Planet Earth. Me? I happen to think there is a God. It gives me some hope to believe there is something smarter and better than the idiots I've met so far in my life down here. Of course, with all the star wars happening almost nightly now before my very eyes, I'm starting to believe the whole Trinity theory is coming back to bite us in the ass, with the High Holies pissed off, throwing punches at each other and raining hot rocks down on Roma.

Little Ivan said it best when we were talking outside the general store once. "Billy, all these people who act so smart like they know everything, not-a-one of them knows what's going to happen next. Nobody knows anything about that until we die and move on to some place better, or worse, or maybe just drift into nothingness, game over. Nobody knows."

Ivan, he's the only person in town who thinks for himself, except for me. I wonder if Ivan has noticed what's going on with the Dippers and Polaris.

There goes one now, Big Dipper shooting at Little Dipper, and wait for it...there, Polaris lets out two blue shooters at both Big and Little. It will take maybe five to ten minutes for the shrapnel to fall from the sky. Then someone in town will notice the fires burning up here and they'll send Chief Ridley and his crew who will show up about an hour later to try to put out the fires and blame me and a few other Roma kids for starting them. Funny how nobody ever notices it's the rocks that are burning, there's never any wood. It's not your normal fire. Riddle me this, oh town leaders of Roma– how did us dumb, juvenile delinquent kids get these rocks to burn so blue hot? NASA can't even do that. When they finally do show up, I'll just retreat into my invisible stone hut and enjoy the show of our keystone cops trying to douse these flaming torpedoes sent down from the heavens by our pissed off Trinity who have taken to throwing thunderbolts at their misbehaved children. I just don't see how me getting my high school diploma is going to make any real difference in the outcome of this cosmic calamity.

Here they come screaming down, just like I said they would. Holy shit, these are the biggest ones I've seen yet. Look at that blue chunk. Just change course about two miles and it makes a direct hit on Roma. Let me see them blame that on Billy Burkenstock and his crew.

"Quite the show tonight, huh Billy?" I hear a voice speaking from the darkness just outside the stone hut entrance, but I don't see anyone.

"I can't figure out why they keep hitting this same area, the holler is what we used to call it, now it's the hollow. Any ideas Billy?"

"Who is that? Who's out there? I had nothing to do with this. It's them up there lobbing hot rocks at us for being bad and mean to each other."

"Calm down, Billy. It's only me, Ivan, and I'm not here to arrest you or anything. In fact, I owe you an apology. I thought it was you setting these fires so I followed you up here to see for myself. Lucky for me I hung around long enough to catch my first star show. How long has this been going on?"

"Little Ivan, that you? Come on in the hut so nobody sees you out there. Chief Ridley and his posse will be here soon enough to put out the fires, or more like watch them burn. Get inside here."

Of course Ivan's the one to find his way up here and witness all of this for himself. I've always said Little Ivan's the smartest guy in town. Ivan's a dwarf. That big head of his understands lots of things all the others don't.

"Don't worry Billy, I won't tell anyone about your hideout. They'll never find it either. Not the way you've covered up the entrance with all this brush. Look out. Here come three more streamers. Aren't you afraid they'll make a direct hit on your hiding place?"

"Nah, they're going the other way Ivan, down the mountain heading toward Roma. I've thought about telling them what's happening at one of those town meetings, but I know the Chief and Mayor Mary would just try to pin the blame on me. You know, they'd kill the messenger. I just can't believe that you and me, Ivan, just the two of us, we're the only people in Roma, and maybe anywhere in the world, who have noticed what is going on. I'm glad you're seeing this too, Ivan. Now I know for sure it's not the weed playing with my mind."

"You've fixed this place up pretty nice, Billy. I used to come up here way back when I was a kid. I'd hike up, bring dinner with me and sleep in one of those bunk beds. That one right over there, third row upper bunk, that was mine because it was the darkest."

"I like the one across from it for the same reason, Ivan, and it's the farthest from the door. I pretty much sleep here every weeknight, then clear out and go home on weekends so mom and dad see me around just enough not to wonder what I'm up to. They never even notice I'm not around during the week. I love this place. Never even thought anyone else knew about it. I come and go through that back door and keep the front entrance covered so nobody notices there's anything here."

"Funny thing, Billy, all those years ago I thought I had discovered it too. This was my getaway. I put that camouflage canvas up so the sunlight wouldn't wake me too early in the morning. You know, they built this hut back in the 1930s during the Depression to put kids to work, mostly country kids who were hanging out, doing nothing and causing trouble. It was called the Civilian Conservation Corps and it was run by the army. The kids were treated like little soldiers. They did all kinds of cool stuff like planting trees, clearing hiking trails, building huts and shelters like this one, your stone hut. The way things are now around Roma, around the whole country, I think they ought to bring those Conservation Corps back just to fix everything that's broken and get people working again."

"I'd like that, Ivan. The problem with being a kid in Roma is there's nothing to do. Every day is filled with nothingness. It's worse than boredom, there's not even anything to be bored with."

"The trick is to get up and go, Billy, just leave here, first chance you get. Go somewhere else and reinvent yourself. You can always come back and visit. Roma's not going anywhere. The town's not what it once was, but she's still standing. Lots of other towns aren't. I've noticed over the years, the people who stay here, the ones who never leave, never go out and explore the world, they end up the angry ones, Billy. They become people who can never find any happiness. It's because they never left. It's not just 'Go West Young Man' anymore Billy, it's more like go north, south, east or west, but dear God, please go somewhere. Just get the hell out of your hometown."

"When did you leave here, Ivan? It couldn't have been easy for you."

"Why? Because I'm a dwarf? It's okay Billy, I've already noticed. I'm a full-grown dwarf and proud of it. I moved to Boston the day after I graduated from Roma High School. When my mom died I came back to sell our house, but since it was all paid for and my early memories were here, I decided to keep it as my country getaway. Roma's only about three hours from Boston, so it's easy to drive up or take the train here. Just pick a place and go there, Billy. Move forward and good things happen. Stay still and nothing happens.

That's what you're feeling now. Go backward and uh-oh, only bad things happen. Life really is that simple, Billy, it's like a big shooting range where the hardest target to hit is the moving one. Look over there, Billy, here comes another streamer, even bigger than the last one. Can you see it, just to the right of the notch?"

"It's a blue one, Ivan, so it came out of Polaris. They always look like they're headed straight for the hut when they're coming down, then they dip into the hollow. Too bad Chief Ridley isn't down there looking around with his posse. They could finally see one hit and then try to explain how Roma's kids made that happen. They are beautiful to watch come down aren't they, Ivan."

"They sure are, Billy, until you think about it and understand how just one big one with a direct hit could destroy all of Roma, hell our entire planet if it was large enough."

"Yeah, that part isn't so beautiful. I've got this idea, Ivan, that the High Holy Trinity up there are all pissed off at us, and at each other, so they're heaving flaming rocks which are raining down on us. Why they're all landing right here, I haven't quite figured that out yet."

"Hmmm...that sure is some pretty deep space thinking there, Billy. I'm not saying you're right, I'm not saying you're wrong, but it would explain a lot of things that have been going on lately. We've been heading downhill at a fast clip. Take your pick: culture, country, community–Roma's just a local example of the whole world's downfall. You think the gods, or God, might be pissed off, huh? Makes sense to me, I like it. Even God must get fed up with all the bullshit we dish out."

"Yeah, Ivan, that's what I'm saying. But why now? And why are you and me the only two people noticing it? Hear that, Ivan? The whiz and then the thud, that's the last one hitting. That one sounded even closer. C'mon, let's go see the blue flame. It's way hotter than any fire you've ever felt before."

"It's snowing pretty hard out there now. That should put the fires out quickly."

"No way, Ivan, these rock fires from outer space burn for hours, even days...doesn't matter if it rains, snows, sleets or hails. This one's the biggest one I've seen yet. But the snow coming down now will keep Chief Ridley and his crew away. They never hike in when the weather's this bad. Look at that rock, Ivan, I've never seen anything shaped like that before. How about you?"

"No, I haven't ever seen anything like it. You're right about the heat too. Never felt this hot before, it's like a sauna out here. How many of these fires have you seen, Billy?"

"Over the last two years, probably about fifty. They started out as just little rocks about the size of baseballs, then kept getting bigger and bigger. You want some of this? I always light one up whenever another space rock hits. It's my very own welcome ritual to the Gods."

"Sure, I'll take a puff or two. Be disrespectful not to, right? I mean it is a welcome ritual. I like to smoke a little when I'm making my rounds at the museum. That's what I do in Boston, Billy, I'm the night watchman at the Fine Arts Museum. I walk around all night long, listening to music, talking to the beautiful paintings and admiring the sculptures. It's just me and the art for twelve hours of tranquility, the perfect job for me, Billy. That's important too. You've got to find the right job for you, one that makes you happy, at peace with yourself."

"I wondered what that uniform was for; seems like you're always wearing it whenever I see you around town. Makes you look official, Ivan, like you're in charge of something. I thought maybe you were a doorman at one of those big Boston hotels. But a museum guard, that's even better. You know what, Ivan? With this storm getting even worse you probably shouldn't be walking down the mountain road tonight. I have an extra sleeping bag and pillow in the stone hut. How about you stay up here with me tonight? I always sleep great up here...sometimes twelve, even fifteen hours."

"If it's okay with you, Billy, I'd like that. She's your hut now. I don't mind the hike down, but it probably will be better in the morning. You have anything to eat up here?"

"You hungry, Ivan? I've got all kinds of food stashed up here. We can toast marshmallows on our meteor fire and make s'mores. That'll be our desert. We'll have peanut butter and honey on raisin bread toast for our main course, with an appetizer of teriyaki beef jerky, compliments of Rufus and his general store. I have apple cider too. Dinner's covered. It'll be nice to have someone else to eat with for a change."

That night turned into another, and then another. In the end we were snowed in for three days. We had plenty of food, though I have to say, Ivan ate all my teriyaki jerky and most of the peanut butter too. But it was worth it, probably the best three days of my life. We played cards, and Ivan taught me how to play chess. He carries a miniature chess board with him; Ivan says you never know when you're going to meet someone who wants to play a game. We talked a lot.

I like talking to Ivan. He's like that super smart little brother I never had, even though he's way older than me, way wiser too. He's got his own theories about lots of things. His big one is how we can make miracles happen for other people but not for ourselves. Ivan makes lots of miracles happen every day. He listened to my ideas, and he never laughed at a single one of them. Ivan's the only grownup I've ever met who actually listens and hears at the same time.

That third morning, the snow finally stopped. I woke up around ten and saw that Ivan was gone. I knew it even before I looked over at his bunk because I couldn't hear his snoring. Ivan sure can snore. But I liked hearing it at night, knowing he was over there sleeping in his favorite bunk. He left a note on the empty peanut butter jar saying, 'Billy- it's time to get back to my museum, to my paintings. Thanks for the hospitality. Keep your eyes on the Dippers and Polaris until I get back in a few weeks...and get some more peanut butter. Ivan'

I saw his little footprints outside the door. They went for only ten steps then disappeared. Strange that. The night before Ivan left I had a dream. Ivan and I were sleeping up here in the stone hut when three enormous red, green and blue flaming boulders came screaming down from the heavens–one from Big Dipper, one from Little Dipper and the third one, the biggest, came from Polaris. It was like the High Holies had finally decided to stop fighting each other and instead focus their almighty wrath on us, Planet Earth, their misbehaving water rock.

These three huge screamers were headed right for Roma, which was already burning blue. But Ivan and me, we were safe, tucked away all warm and cozy in our stone hut carved into the side of our mountain fortress. I woke up suddenly in a cold sweat, gasping for air, afraid it was really happening. But it was just a bad dream. Wasn't it?

# I AM GOD

Did you see that piece in the Globe last week? The one about the statue of Adam mysteriously shattering into pieces on the patio floor at the museum? I was mentioned, well kind of. In the third column, the writer says a security guard discovered the fallen apple-eater on Sunday night. That's me. I'm the graveyard security guard, the entire nighttime surveillance team at Boston's Museum of Fine Arts, the fourth largest museum in the whole country. Isn't that ridiculous? With all the masterpieces, beauty and wealth contained in this one building, the museum makes budget cuts to the single most important area of operations...SECURITY. I tell you, of all the things to steal in this world, art, major art, is probably the easiest. Why that is, I do not know.

My name is Ivan—Ivan Ambrose Goddinski. My mother was a Russian gypsy who met my father, a Rumanian Jew, during the Battle of Stalingrad in World War II. They hid out and shtupped their way through that bloody battle, when the Russians defeated Hitler's feared sixth Army and really turned World War II around. Even though America takes credit for winning World War II, it was really the Russians who broke Hitler's stranglehold on Europe, with that one long scorched-earth battle over what once was, Stalingrad.

I'm thirty years at the Museum now, been here longer than anyone else on the security staff. I moved to Boston the day after I graduated from Roma High School and started working at the museum a few months later. Some people might say it's a shitty job, but I love it. Doesn't pay much, just $33,333.33 a year, but I do get to work alone, which I love. I'm surrounded every night by truly beautiful, powerful, awe-inspiring works of art: Rembrandt, Chagall, Picasso, Renoir, Degas, Lautrec…they're all here, and I get to watch over them. I consider it an honor to guard these treasures, and I do take it seriously. Every Thursday through Monday night, and even Tuesday and Wednesday if they happen to call me in, here I am from 8pm to 8am, walking these sacred hallways, worshipping these paintings, sculptures and statues that hold the power to make life worth living.

Beauty is a funny thing, it truly is in the eye of the beholder. Look at me for instance. I'm barely four feet tall with an oversized head, huge hands and short legs, which classifies me as a dwarf. I weigh about one-hundred-sfifty pounds. For a man of my stature that's probably about forty pounds too heavy. So physically, I may not fit into your classical image of what you might call beautiful, or even handsome. But if you can just look beyond the surface, which most people can't, I am a definite masterpiece. My mother used to call me her little David. But I was well into my thirties when she was still saying that.

That Globe story quotes Henry Huntington, I call him the Hoser, as the museum's chief spokesman. That's pure fiction. Hoser's one of those trust funders who has never really worked a day in his life. You know the type. His mommy is on the Board, so little Henry gets a title and an office but never does a damn thing. The Hoser doesn't like me either. He'd love to fire me, but he can't because I'm too damn important around here. I'm a technical whiz at video surveillance. I can set up cameras in nooks and crannies nobody would ever suspect, then pump the video feed back into our control room where one person can oversee the entire museum through twelve television monitors. Hoser loves that setup because it let him cut security staff to save money, and made him a hero to his mommy. I felt bad for the daytime security staff he let go last year, but at the time there wasn't anything I could do about it. Now things have changed since Adam lost his balance. I hear Hoser's mother ordered him to hire back all the security staff he let go plus three more just for insurance purposes. In fact, I heard it first hand. I listened in on the phone call from the control room. I love surveillance technology. It truly is the next best thing to being there, sometimes even better.

What Hoser doesn't realize is I've got cameras set up that he knows nothing about–in his office, his private bathroom and the boardroom too. I'm everywhere. I like to know everything that's going on in my museum. I feed the video through a secure line on the master panel only I have access to. When I come in for work, first thing I do is review the footage to catch up on what Hoser's been doing in my absence. Usually it's not very much, but I need to see all and know all, because around here I AM GOD, and this museum is my Garden of Eden. So you can understand why Adam had to take the fall, again.

I mean it…I AM GOD. Not only at my museum but to everyone and everything I know. I make things happen, real things for real people. I don't mean in some loosey-goosey, let's all hug each other, sing me Kumbaya and I'll turn my other cheek kind of way. I'm talking action; I make miracles happen, real stuff, not that pie-in-the-sky, someday we'll understand it all crap.

I remember the exact moment it hit me, like a right cross thrown from nowhere, almost ten years ago. That night,

I was patrolling the third-floor gallery, enjoying a rich ruby-red Burgundy whilst listening to Beethoven's thundering ninth symphony. You know the one, DE DE DE DE DE DE DE DE, BOOM BOOM BOOM BOOM BOOM, BOOMBOOM. Supposedly, he went crazy writing it. I can believe that, because it's way beyond anything anybody in this world could create in a normal state of mind. Clearly, the musical angels were screaming heavenly notes into both of Beethoven's ears. Of course he went deaf.

There I was, admiring Rembrandt's epic "The Angel and the Prophet Balaam" painted in 1626. In it, Rembrandt shows a protective angel guiding Balaam through a ferocious, bloody battle. Now, Balaam's not worried about himself in the painting. Oh no, he's kicking ass and saving the lives of everyone around him. It came to me right then and there. I must have looked at that canvas for three straight hours, right through to the end of my shift, with Beethoven's ninth thundering over and over and over. We've got it all wrong. We always have.

For five thousand some odd years—whenever you want to date civilization back to—everyone's been sitting around, praying to God, waiting for God to make miracles happen, to make everything better. Look at all the paintings. It's so clear. From the Egyptians to the Greeks, to the Romans to the Renaissance, to today...they are all about people praying to something, to someone they can't see or hear, then wondering why nothing good ever happens, why miracles go AWOL and bad shit continues to rule the roost.

Like a cold slap in the face, it woke me up right then and there. The answer is so simple. Everything's simple once you get it, once you see it for what it really is. We've just become blinded and powerless over the years. Here's the truth...WE ARE THE MIRACLE MAKERS. We are GOD for everyone else but ourselves; not in some pray for me, offer it up, keep the faith, God is good kind of way. I'm talking about food, shelter, sex, power, success, fame, fortune—real things in the world we live in. Not that—better luck next time, maybe in your afterlife, see-you-later-sucker bullshit. We can make real things happen for real people who can't make these things happen for themselves, and that my friend is called a true miracle.

I'm not talking about nepotism. I hate nepotism, and cronyism too. Handing out the good jobs, expensive toys and big fancy houses to family and friends is what's killing this country, destroying our culture and making good people give up on even trying. Nepotism and cronyism form the root of all mediocrity; there really should be harsh laws against them. Henry the Hoser, for instance, would be doing a life sentence, his mother too, ideally in the same cell. No, I'm talking about making unseen miracles happen for people you're not related to, for people you don't even really know. That's how God is supposed to work, strong and silent. He doesn't care about who's connected through friends and family. He's an equal opportunity God, supposedly.

Last Sunday, I got in just before eight and went right to my private video stash to see what the Hoser's been up to. I couldn't believe my eyes, or my ears. Hoser's got some bimbo in his office, telling her she can start in two weeks, soon as he lets go of Miss Callahan, our Renaissance Restoration expert. He's got this twenty-something Rockette dancing on his lap, promising her a position, probably many positions, at the expense of my favorite coworker, the woman I watch over, albeit from a distance. I'll focus in closer, there. Like the Irishman's song says, "She's an angel in the first degree."

I mean, look at her. I'll go in just a little closer, a little more focus. Perfecto. Look at those red curls, her big blue eyes so dreamy behind those giant framed glasses she wears when she's working. She is a masterpiece, and I mean that respectfully, of course. I love to watch her work. Her dedication to the craft, the purity of her restorative technique…she is high art in the first degree. I know she'd be mad if she knew I stuck a camera, or two, in her studio, but it's for her own good. Uh-oh, she's getting ready to go. I've got to run now. I like to be at the door to say goodnight. Now, with Adam needing her tender loving care after his fall from grace last week, I guess Eve Callahan's going to be working nights and weekends for at least the next three years, maybe five. Who knows? I hear Hoser even raised her salary. GOD knows she deserved one.

Do you see why it had to be done? Adam was a sinner. He had to be sacrificed so that Eve could stay in my Garden of Eden. Everything's so simple once you see it clearly. As miracles go, this one was a cakewalk. All it took was my Power-Spray water gun turned up to maximum strength, that's 90 pounds of water pressure, trained on Adam's groin area for twelve seconds. He never had a chance. Down he went, body parts everywhere. I turned up the heat and waited five and a half hours until all the water dried up to officially discover this disastrous incident. Then I called the Hoser at home with the bad news. Our roving first floor camera failed to pick up any irregular activity. The cause remains an unsolved mystery. Oh, here comes my angel now. God she's beautiful…

"Goodnight, Mr. Goddinsky. I'll see you tomorrow."

"Goodnight Miss Callahan." And tomorrow, and tomorrow, and the next day too, because GOD watches over Eve Callahan in the form of me, Ivan Ambrose Goddinski.

## PUT ME IN COACH

Shiloh and her Mom moved to Roma almost a year ago in late August, just in time to start school. In a small town like Roma, newcomers always stand out. Everyone wanted to know everything about them. Folks in Roma can be downright charming when they want information from you. Once they get what they want, not so much.

It always starts with the check-you-out dinner or barbecue. You get invited over for what is usually a pretty good meal during which you get pelted with nosy, personal-business questions. Then once the third degree is all done and they have what they need to attach a label to the newbies, they give you dessert to go, and tell everyone what they found out. Shiloh and her mother were just a little too much for the inquisitors to process or label, so they just decided to hate them from the very start. When it came out that Shiloh played basketball and was pretty good at it, that presented a real problem for some of the nosiest families in Roma. Foul number one, just for being different so early in the game.

The Garons moved to Roma from Montreal, so you can call that foul number two, as Quebecois Canadians were never very popular in these parts. Roma traces its roots back to German, Austrian, and Swedish heritage—not French Canadian. But that wasn't the clincher. Shiloh Garon and her beautiful mother, Simone, were of Metis heritage. They descended from a mixed marriage many years ago between a French colonial trapper and an aboriginal woman, to produce mixed race or Metis children. Today there are about half a million Metis living in Canada, mostly out in the western provinces. But any way you cut it, and whatever name you call it, Shiloh and Simone Garon just didn't fit the Roma mold. They never would, no matter what they did or how hard they tried.

Simone had married an American, a Vermonter in fact, who grew up in Roma. They had lived together happily with their young daughter for ten years until one morning Shiloh woke up and daddy was gone. He left a brief note on the kitchen table saying he was moving up north to the Territories, which one he didn't say, and that he would send for them when he got set up. They never did hear from him again.

The Roma gatekeepers of new arrivals were usually low-level social butterflies desperate to be invited and included in every event and party happening in town. They were overwhelmed by the Garons, by the life they had already lived and the stories they were happy to share, holding absolutely nothing back. Word was out before the dinner dishes were done that night, the Garons were going to be a problem—Simone to the Moms because she was beautiful; Shiloh to the girls because she had game. There was a new kid in town and she could play basketball, for real. Foul number three, just for being too damn good, and the season hadn't even started.

As it happens, I was the girls' varsity basketball coach when Shiloh Garon came to town. I was also the head janitor at the high school. Strange combination that. In my former life, before retiring to Vermont, I coached some pretty good teams to championships down in New York City. When Roma's former coach suddenly had to resign in mid-season for reasons not disclosed, which usually means he was fired,

Principal Barrows offered me the position just to fill out the schedule. That was three seasons and far too many heartbreaking losses ago.

Roma used to be known for having excellent teams in all sports, especially basketball. We were the Roma Centurions, and we were feared, in Division III. Of course, Roma used to be known for lots of things we're not known for today. Too many families have moved away, back to the big cities. The kids who stayed just aren't as athletic as Roma kids used to be. My starting five on varsity, my only five, have played together since the sixth grade. That's both a blessing and a curse. They did alright on the middle-school level, even went undefeated one year in the eighth grade, but when they hit high school they just couldn't keep up with the other schools' athleticism and team play. Our girls always have plenty of attitude. They think they're something special, but they just can't ever score enough points to win any big games against good teams. They always play well against the bad teams, beating them by twenty points, like bullies taking out their frustrations on the weaker kids. But put them up against a real team with true talent and solid fundamentals and it's game over, they don't want to play anymore. When Shiloh hit town just in time for our new season, I thought maybe, just maybe, we finally had the makings of a real team. Perhaps we could even win a championship. Things took a turn, though, down a much darker road.

By the time of our opening game against Turnbridge Academy, it was clear that Shiloh was our best player, by far. She had a great outside shot from every angle that never seemed to miss. She dribbled circles around and between the legs of anyone who tried to guard her. Her quickness gave her an easy layup any time she felt like driving to the hoop. She was a great passer to anyone who could get open and catch the ball. When I announced the starting lineup after practice the night before our first game with Shiloh at point guard, the senior girls didn't take it well. They even looked surprised.

"But Coach, that's Emily's position. She's always been our point guard." Nella Dobber, nicknamed 'Elbows' by me because of the way she throws them around and gets into foul trouble early, had her arm around Emily who was already crying on her shoulder.

"You can't start a freshman, who's not even from here, ahead of Emily. We're seniors this year, Coach. This is our team." Nella averaged barely four points and three rebounds last year, but when it came to defending her lifelong friend Emily, she was always tenacious.

"It's been your team the last three years, Elbows, and all we have to show for it is losing records. I think with Shiloh bringing the ball up and passing it around to all of you, we're going to be a better team, and you're going to score more points. Wouldn't it be fun to win a few more games, maybe even beat some good teams for a change?"

"But we don't need her to do it coach, that's for sure. We can do it by ourselves, nobody else." Julie Dawson was red-faced and raised her voice with each word. I called her 'Sasquatch', not because she had big feet but because she couldn't dribble to save her life, always bouncing the ball off her left foot sending it out of bounds.

"You girls went four and twelve last year. Sasquatch, you averaged five points a game, and sadly you were our highest scorer. Emily and Elbows never got you the ball. They couldn't even get the ball past half court against any of the better teams. Wouldn't you like to score more than five points a game, Sasquatch? Maybe ten or twenty even. We just might win every game if you do." I could see Sasquatch liked the idea of scoring more points by the way her eyes glazed over and how she fell silent while looking at her left foot.

Then our forwards chimed in. They both played miserably last season but loved sending game photos of themselves, taken by their mothers, into our local newspaper. I called them Frik and Frak because they were always together and liked to finish each other's sentences, just like an old couple.

"I thought last season was a breakthrough season for us. Yes, we did only have four wins, Coach. But many of our losses were by less than fifteen." Funny thing was, Frik, aka Jill Lacking, truly thought that was a positive sign.

"Many? Maybe two were by less than fifteen points. The rest were by twenty or more. We were the Bad News Bears of Division III Girls Basketball, in Vermont no less. I don't think you can get any less competitive than that. Now, we have a real player who can help us come together and win as a team. How can this be bad news, and why is Whispers still crying?"

My nickname for Emily Anders was 'Whispers', because she never spoke to me directly but instead whispered to the other girls, who would convey her message, unless it was a real secret. Thus the name Whispers. They were more of a group therapy session than an actual team. But I was determined that was going to change.

"That's a bit mean, Coach, and I'm going to tell my mother what you said. We are good basketball players and we're a great team because we are friends. It's just that the refs

are always against us and you're not coaching us right."
Frak's mother was the Athletic Director at Roma High School.
It was a volunteer position but wielded a certain amount of
local clout with parents who wanted their kids to get more
playing time. Frak, Joan Doolittle, hadn't made a single foul
shot in three years, usually missing the entire backboard.
Going into this season, she'd missed forty-two free throws in
a row, a high school record I'm sure, maybe even a world
record."

"Not coaching you right, Frak...interesting. What do
you think I should be doing differently? Please, do enlighten
me." Of course, Frik jumped in.

"Well you shouldn't be calling us names like the Bad
News Bees for one thing."

"Bears."

"What?"

"It's the Bad News Bears. That's what I called you. It's
from an old movie about a baseball team that was bad, so very
bad, until a really good player showed up, joined the team
and turned their season around. Hmmm, I wonder if that
could happen in real life, in Roma for instance." I left out the
part about the coach in the movie being a raging alcoholic.

Like the tag team they are, Frak took over. "Whatever,
it's not a very nice thing to say and probably not a very good
movie either. You should not be starting her. She's an
outsider. She only just moved to Roma, and nobody even likes
her."

"Coach." Shiloh had been sitting on the bleachers
listening to all of this while spinning a basketball on her
middle finger. "You don't have to start me, I can just come off

the bench. The girls sound like they have Turnbridge handled. I'm ready to play when you need me."

"I can't believe what I'm hearing. This isn't a tea party where we only invite the people who agree with us. This is a basketball team, the best players available are the ones who will play. What have I said at the start of every season? My golden rule, cronyism never wins big games and it always loses championships. Well, I think we've proven that for the last three seasons girls. Now, we have a chance to change for the better. Shiloh, you're our starting point guard tomorrow night. That's my decision, and it is final. You earned the position. Emily, you'll see plenty of playing time coming off the bench for Elbows."

"Me? Why are you subbing Emily in for me?"

"Because Elbows, you two are besties, and you both happen to be guards. I seem to remember last season you were in early foul trouble in every single game. Now I can sit you down and put in Whispers when you get called for three fouls in two minutes. Problem solved, any more questions or concerns, girls? Good. Now everyone, go home and get a good night's sleep. Let's kick some Turnbridge ass tomorrow. I have a good feeling about this game."

"I'm telling my mom you said 'ass', and stop calling me Frak."

Turns out I shouldn't have had a good feeling at all. I should have felt an extreme case of heartburn coming on. Really, I should have seen it all coming. I just underestimated the hatred seething inside these All-American clean-cut Roma girls. I had noticed in our scrimmages how they refused to pass the ball to Shiloh, or even warn her when she was about to run into a screen. Whenever she scored there were never any high-fives. I just put it all down to Shiloh being a freshman and having to earn the seniors' respect. But it was much uglier than that. They did not want this outsider playing on what they considered to be 'their' team, or even in 'their' town. They were determined not to include her, to make her invisible. That's a fourth foul against Shiloh, and it's an ugly one. We'll call it, exclusion.

That evening I received phone calls, emails and texts from all the parents, Principal Barrows, and of course from Frak's mother, our volunteer Athletic Director, Anna Doolittle. It was like they were all reading from the same script, and that script said Emily Anders must start against Turnbridge Academy and Shiloh Garon was not a good representation of our town and school. They sounded downright religious in the passion of their message. With each call, I drank another beer with an equal amount of fervor, followed by a tequila shooter. I was channeling my very best Walter Matthau and feeling pretty good about our chances of beating Turnbridge.

I listened, and I listened, and then I listened some more. To each parent I ended the communication by simply saying, "I am the coach of this team and I will play the best players. As I told your kids at the end of practice today, I will not tolerate cronyism anymore." I could hear them screaming as I hung up and signed off. Cronies hate it when you point the finger at what they're doing, not just in Roma but everywhere. This season was going to be different. I was going to show these girls and their parents that not everything in life is rigged. It doesn't matter who barbecues with whom. What matters most in sports, especially high school sports, is athletic ability and love for the game. Shiloh had both going for her, and she showed it to everyone against Turnbridge in that first game.

From the opening whistle, she was amazing out there, an unstoppable force all over the court. The stands were packed with Roma fans and parents. But you could have heard that proverbial pin drop every time Shiloh scored for Roma, followed by a deafening silence. Then, when one of the other girls made a basket, off a perfect pass from Shiloh, the stands would erupt with applause. Even the Turnbridge coach looked over at me wondering what was going on. We beat Turnbridge by fifteen points, the same margin they had beaten us by last season.

The next week we went on to beat Trusca and Siena Falls, two teams we hadn't beaten in four years. Shiloh was averaging twenty-five points and ten steals a game. Even better, she was dishing out nearly twenty assists per game. All the girls were scoring off laser passes from Shiloh. It was easy—they would go to their favorite spots as Shiloh dribbled the ball up, then she'd hit them with a perfect pass for a wide-open shot. That's fundamental basketball at its best.

My phone stopped ringing at night. The emails and texts stopped piling up. Everyone seemed to be happy because we were winning. Frik and Frak stopped complaining and started playing some team defense. Frak even hit three foul shots in a row at Trusca, thus ending her record streak for most consecutive misses, which I am sure will stand for many years in Vermont, perhaps even nationwide. Elbows hadn't fouled out of a single game and was starting to hit some of those three-pointers she liked to throw up. Sasquatch was pulling down ten rebounds per game and scoring four or five baskets from underneath. Even

Whispers was chipping in, coming off the bench to score four points and hand out four assists in each game. We were starting to look and play like a team, though we were only three games into the season. The one real problem was, whenever I took Shiloh out, even for a brief rest, it all seemed to fall apart. They just went back to their old ways and played horrible one-on-one basketball.

I stopped resting Shiloh, and we kept on winning. Our next three games: Roma 58-Winston 50, Roma 62-Barbarville 52, Roma 55-Vandalburg 52, and the Vandals were in the state finals last year. We were six wins and no losses, and still none of the girls would recognize Shiloh as the reason for our turnaround. They wouldn't even talk to her. In all my years of coaching, both boys and girls basketball, I'd never seen anything like the treatment Shiloh received from these supposedly upstanding Roma girls. I was amazed how Shiloh never let their ugly behavior affect her game. She just wanted to play basketball. Shiloh knew how to score. She knew how to win. She just kept getting better with every game. Foul number five on Shiloh, for daring to play above them all.

It was the Wellsboro game that brought out the true colors of the girls, and even worse, their parents. Wellsboro was the perennial powerhouse in our little mountain league. They were Division III state champions four years in a row, and like us, were undefeated in six games. This matchup was a big Friday night event. Everyone wanted to see us play as a preview to the state championship in six weeks. Wellsboro's coach was Vermont basketball legend Prudy DuMont, a six-foot-four-inch hothead who played power forward for the University of South Carolina, and even played one year in the WNBA before tearing up both of her knees on an awkward landing after an attempted dunk, which she missed. That was the end of Prudy's short-lived professional career and the beginning of her highly successful high school coaching career. The rumor mill was buzzing about this being Coach Prudy's final year at Wellsboro. After this season she was moving on to coach college basketball. Wouldn't a fifth straight championship make the perfect parting gift for Coach Prudy? Not in my mind.

We were behind from the opening tip. Coach Prudy had done her scouting and her strategy was easy to see—deny Shiloh the ball and make the other girls score. I would have done the same. Wellsboro defenders had Shiloh double-teamed on her dribble down court, with a third player floating the inside passing lane. The other girls were doing what they do best, passing to each other. But nobody was scoring, or even taking shots. Every time Shiloh passed the ball off, she never got it back. We were down by ten at the end of the first period, then eighteen by the half. The only reason it was even that close was because Shiloh had eight steals, which she turned into sixteen points on breakaway layups. At halftime I was pretty pissed off and let the girls know about it.

"I don't know what you think you're doing out there, but you're not playing team basketball. Shiloh's the only one scoring. We've got sixteen points and they're all hers. Get open, and when she passes you the ball for God's sake catch it and shoot. Don't just stand there looking at it. Take the shot or pass it off. It's really not that hard, girls."

"She's not making good passes, Coach." Sasquatch had taken two wide-open shots. Both had sailed over the backboard.

"You missed two easy ones, Sasquatch. I could have hit them with one eye closed. Shiloh's playing one on nine out there so far. If you girls decide to show up and start playing like I know you can, we can still beat this team. Frik, Frak, you have one rebound between the two of you. I don't even know who got it. If you're not going to score, or even take a shot, you at least have to grab some rebounds and play some defense."

"Maybe you should put Emily in. At least they won't double-team her, and she can make better passes to us." Elbows had never given up the fight to get her bestie Whispers back into her starting guard position. I looked over and saw the smirk on Whispers' face. Right then in that moment, I understood what she was doing. Whispers had told the girls not to play well, and as always, to deny Shiloh the ball.

"Of course, they're not going to double-team her, Elbows, they're not afraid of Whispers scoring. They'll just take the ball away from her on the dribble and then you'll never get any passes. Is that what you want? No. Here's what we're going to do. Elbows, you're out."

"What? I only have three fouls, Coach."

"You're out, Elbows, and your bestie friend is in. Can you tell her that, as she doesn't seem to be able to speak to me, not even a whisper. Your only job, Whispers, is to bring the ball down with Shiloh. By that I mean, don't try to dribble, just catch the inbound pass, and when Shiloh breaks, pass it back to her. Frik, Frak, Sasquatch, if there are three players defending Shiloh, at least one of you has got to be open. Hell, all of you should be open. Just catch the ball and take the shot. That's really the essence of this beautiful game of basketball, just catch and release. It's like fishing, only with a ball. I think we're lucky to be down by only eighteen. We can make that up in five minutes if we play like a team. Now, let's go out there and win this game, as a team"

"But Coach..."

"Bench, Elbows, and be ready. We may need you in the final minutes."

We were a whole new team coming out of halftime. Shiloh took over, slashing inside for floating layups, getting to the foul line and hitting jumpers from everywhere. Frik and Frak hit a basket each and finally started grabbing some rebounds. Sasquatch had four points. Even Whispers stuck to the game plan and passed the ball right back to Shiloh bringing it down court. At the end of the third period we were behind 44-40, and the Wellsboro players were arguing with each other about whose fault it was. We'd held them to only ten points while scoring twenty-two since halftime. Shiloh had fourteen of those points, which gave her thirty for the game. Even better, we were playing as a team.

The whole fourth period our Roma gym was rocking. We tied it up then fell behind by two, then four, then Sasquatch hit a three, Frik put back a rebound and we were up by one. Then they came right back and scored again. Sasquatch was boxing out and grabbing rebounds like I'd never seen her do before. She'd get fifteen rebounds in that second half, ten in the fourth period alone.

Coach Prudy over on the Wellsboro bench was going crazy, screaming at her girls to deny Shiloh the ball. Then she'd holler at the refs that they weren't calling any fouls on us. Then, not to be left out, Prudy blew up at her assistant coach, shoving her, saying the girls weren't running any of her plays right.

With two minutes to go and the score tied, Coach Prudy turned to the bleachers and told everyone, including the Wellsboro fans, to "shut the fuck up." She threw an open water bottle then picked up a chair and was ready to launch it into the stands until her assistants managed to wrestle it away. It was a legendary meltdown, one that I would have enjoyed even more if I wasn't caught up in my own moment, coaching to win this game.

With thirty seconds to go, Wellsboro's all-star point guard took a ten-foot jumper, the same one she'd been killing us with the whole game. This time she missed it, and Frak came down with the rebound. Our ball, down by one; I called our final timeout. This was it. We could beat the defending state champion on our home court and remain undefeated. Just one more basket would seal it.

"OK girls, you're playing like the team I knew we could be. This is what it's all about. Great rebound, Frak. Now, here's what we're going to do. We need to kill some time. Whispers, you pass it into Shiloh, then come inbounds and go to the top of the key. Sasquatch, you stay over to the left. Way over. Shiloh, you're over on the right. On the inbound pass, Shiloh you hold the ball. They won't foul you, they've seen what you can do at the line. With ten seconds to go, everyone clear left and, Shiloh, you drive in for the score. They're going to have to get out of your way or foul you. Either way, we win this game, girls."

I did notice Whispers whisper something to Sasquatch as they walked onto the court. A moment later, I knew what that ugly whisper was. She had her own game plan all along. Without hesitation, Whispers threw that inbound pass way over Shiloh's head, all the way across court to Sasquatch, who caught it and then passed it right back to Whispers. Once again, they were freezing Shiloh out.

I was out of timeouts so all I could do was scream at Whispers with the crowd roaring behind me, "Pass it to Shiloh."

The bad news was, Shiloh by this time was double-covered, with a third player, that all-star point guard, floating the passing lane between Whispers and Shiloh. Whispers just stood there at the top of the key, like she was frozen in time, watching the clock tick down—fifteen, fourteen, thirteen, twelve, eleven, ten...at ten seconds she looked over at me with empty eyes and the hollow face of someone who was already hardened by life. She had never spoken to me before, at least not directly, but these words were meant to be heard only by me, for they were aimed at my jugular.

"See, Coach. See what happens when you don't do what you're told. You never were one of us either. You'll always just be the janitor."

That said, Whispers launched a hook shot with just five seconds to go. Whisper's shot never had a chance of going in; she never even looked at the basket, just threw it up. I was surprised it even hit the backboard. But hit it did, and out of nowhere from the right corner came Shiloh, sailing through the air. She grabbed the rebound in midair and tipped it in for the easy put-back, just beating the buzzer.

The ref signaled the basket good and game over. Coach Prudy went even more ballistic, throwing her clipboard, another water bottle, and finally, that chair on to the court. Both teams stood frozen in shock at what had just happened. Whispers collapsed down to her knees in tears. We beat Wellsboro, final score 71-70. Nobody can ever take that away from us. Nobody could ever take that away from Shiloh.

Coach Prudy brushed by, refusing to shake my hand, or even look at me. Shiloh stood beneath the basket, still holding the game ball, looking over at me with that smile she could always muster, even when she understood the ugliness of what was happening all around her. I ran over and gave her a bear hug. The other girls, her teammates, walked away in silence, acting as if they'd just lost instead of beating the four-time state champions on our home court.

"You did it, kid. You beat them all, Shiloh Garon. This is your moment. I'm so damn proud of you."

By the time we made it back to the locker room the other girls had already cleared out. I figured Whispers and Sasquatch just didn't want to hear what I had to say to them about that last play. It could wait until our next practice. I was going to have a heart-to-heart with Whispers for what she said to me. I wasn't even sure how I should respond as I had never dealt with anyone so hateful and disrespectful. But the others, I couldn't understand why they didn't stick around to celebrate our big victory.

The write-up in our weekend newspaper was all about Shiloh and how she beat Wellsboro single-handedly with 44 points, 13 steals, 10 assists and 12 rebounds. A quadruple-double, never before accomplished in Vermont Division III basketball, or II, or I, or even in the WNBA so far as I know. I believe that article was what pushed them and their parents over the edge. They just couldn't bear it to be known that this wasn't their team anymore. Now it was official, even in print, with photos. Shiloh Garon was the reason the Centurions were undefeated and driving toward a state championship, Roma's first in a very long time. They couldn't fool themselves or anyone else anymore...

We waited for them at practice on Monday, Shiloh and me. Three o'clock our usual starting time went by and still no team. Then at three-thirty they started to straggle in, to hand in their uniforms. Frik and Frak showed up first, saying their moms didn't want them to play basketball anymore because school had to come first. In all the years I'd known them, they'd never gotten above a B- in any of their classes. Suddenly their moms wanted them to be co-valedictorians.

As if on cue, Sasquatch marched in just as Frik and Frak left the gym. What, were they lined up outside? Sasquatch's story was a doozy. She told me she wanted to join the school band and basketball was taking up too much of her practice time. Thing was, Sasquatch didn't even play a musical instrument. She had her best game ever against Wellsboro and I could see from the tears in her eyes that she didn't really want to quit, but mommy and daddy were making her.

Elbows came in all hot and heavy, threw her jersey on the court in front of me and said, "You never should have benched me, Coach. Now you don't even have a team to coach."

She picked up a basketball and took one final shot, which of course sailed over the backboard and into the stands. But it was Whispers showing up five minutes later who delivered the parting shot...

"You should have listened to my mom, to all our moms and dads when they called you, Coach. This is our team, my team really. I am the point guard for Roma High

School. I've always been the leader of these girls, and I always will be. Not this outsider, who knows how to play basketball but can't do anything else." I chuckled at that, knowing Shiloh was a straight-A student who already spoke four languages.

"You think I'm funny? Well now you're an outsider too, Coach. You don't belong here in Roma any more than she does. You never did. You still don't get it. To us, it's about who gets to play on the varsity, who gets to wear the uniform and represent Roma. That's all that matters. WE decide who's going to have those high school moments. Not you, and certainly not her. Benching me was your biggest mistake."

With that, Emily 'Whispers' Anders threw her jersey at me, missing of course, and exited the gym with both middle fingers raised. That night, I got the call from Frak's mother, Anna Doolittle, our volunteer Athletic Director. She told me it had been decided in an emergency school board meeting that it was in the best interests of all concerned to cancel the remainder of the girls basketball season. She had already spoken with Principal Barrows, who had agreed. I said we could play the J.V. with Shiloh at point guard and still probably go undefeated, maybe even win the championship. She told me that was not an option, as the junior varsity season was cancelled also. Her last words before hanging up were to tell me my services as basketball coach were no longer required at Roma High School, as there would be no team next year due to budgetary constraints.

I still see Shiloh playing every chance she gets, and I'm still her coach every chance I get. The kid's got talent for the game, and I still have my keys to the gym. After all, I am just the janitor and we always hold the keys to the kingdom.

Drop by any night after eight, and you'll see me and Shiloh out there working on her crossover and three-point shots from everywhere. I still know people from my New York days, people who are now coaching on the college level. They're always looking for basketball players who play for the right, no, who play for the only reason...for love of the game. You can be sure, they've all heard about that talented point guard who forced Coach Prudy into early retirement...and they can't wait to meet Shiloh Garon.

## BUBBA THROWS IT DOWN

"What did you say? What was that you said? Oh, you said something, Bubba. Go ahead, say it again. I dare you. I really want you to say it again."

Didn't say a damn thing, just looking at you, sitting there doing nothing, as usual.

"Me? I'm not doing nothing. I'm thinking. This is how I think, in the sitting down position. You don't always have to be moving to be doing something. This whole always being in motion routine just to look busy is all wrong. That's why nobody ever gets anything done. They're moving around way too much, wasting time and energy."

So you got it all figured out, huh, Stringer?

"There it is again, that condescending attitude you know I don't like. Yeah, Bubba, I got it all figured out...for me at least. The rest can go figure it out for themselves. That's not my business."

Let's get outta here. Let's go do something. There's a town meeting tonight. You know I love those town meetings.

"I'm pretty sure you're banished from all town meetings forever. Yeah, go ahead Bubba, grit your teeth and beat your chest, but three people went to the hospital last time."

Stringer doesn't like to go out much anymore. He just sits around with his collection of bongs watching the news, which makes him even more upset with how bad things are going. He says the country's doing a swan dive straight into the fires of hell and nobody seems to care. Every time that clown of a president with the funny hair and makeup comes

105

on the TV, Stringer says, "somebody go get Nero his fiddle."
Can President Nero really play the fiddle?

"What are you looking at? You want another banana?
Already gave you three. You know I hate those town
meetings, Bubba, just a big waste of time. Always the same
people spouting the same shit. How about we watch *King
Kong* again? You know he almost gets the girl. Ah, quit your
sulking."

Stringer's been in a bad mood ever since he got back
from Vietnam. Yup, Stringer's been pissed off for almost forty
years now. He never was the same after his two tours over
there. Stringer says nobody came back the same, if they were
lucky enough to come back at all. Says he was just way too
young to see what he saw and do what he did. When he got
back to Roma, nothing was the same. All he wanted to do was
smoke pot, watch TV through the night, then sleep all day
long. That's pretty much what Stringer's been doing since the
late seventies.

"The economy's booming, the economy's
booming...they think if they say it enough it will actually come
true. Just like in the *Wizard of Oz*. Truth is, the economy's
tanking. It's clogging the toilet, overflowing the septic and
can't take another flush. Turns out Capitalism is a total sham.
Even the rich folk are starting to complain. These guys must
know that. Where do they find these newscaster clowns? I
swear, a monkey eating a banana could do a better job. No
offense, Bubba."

Yeah, none taken...Stringer grew up in Roma and was
one of the best athletes ever to come out of this little town. Of
course, being the only black guy on the field and playing in
Division III against a bunch of slow white kids from even

smaller towns made it easier. Nobody could keep up with him. But when it came time to graduate, Stringer didn't get any offers to play college ball, or even to go to college at all. There weren't any job offers to work for mommy and daddy or uncle Harry, so Stringer did what guys with no connections always do, he signed up for the Marines and learned how to blow shit up. Big mistake.

"God damn it, Bubba, put down that bong. You know it's my favorite. That's my Buddha bong from Bangkok. Traded everything I was wearing that day for it—boots, jacket, pants, even my wristwatch. Every time I light up, it feels like I'm smoking pure Zen wisdom straight out of Buddha's belly button. So put Buddha down, Bubba, gently. Step away from the Buddha."

Nobody around Roma really talks to Stringer anymore. He's older than most of them who have stuck around. But they all know who he is, a high school legend back in his day. He scored more touchdowns, baskets and goals than anyone else ever did, until that Coughlin kid came along. Stringer was 'The Man' when Roma was still the place to be, before it all started falling to pieces.

"Take your hat and coat off, Bubba, we're not going anywhere. It's still snowing out there, gonna snow all night long, probably tomorrow and the next day too. Go grab us a couple of beers and I'll find Kong."

I didn't know Stringer back in his glory days. I found him after he got back from Vietnam, all broken up and lost.

"See, there they go again talking about how absolutely great everything is. Oh look, unemployment's down again to practically zero. If you're not working, it must be your fault. Truth is, unemployment's down because nobody's looking for work anymore, so they don't count them. Everyone's given up. Soon, there's gonna be just a couple of hundred people working full time and then they'll say we have one-hundred percent employment. Who buys this bullshit? I can't wait till they replace all these jabbering cheerleaders with robots. Then, these talking heads can see just how bad things really are out there on the street with everyone else."

Yeah, Stringer likes to yell at the TV when he's watching his news channels. Better than yelling at people he says. That's the saddest thing about Stringer. He's really a gentle soul who never wanted to hurt anyone but ended up killing a whole bunch of people, women and children too. The night I found him, Stringer was sitting in front of the TV with his Buddha bong fired up, an empty bottle of Jack Daniels on the floor and a .45 caliber pistol stuck in his mouth. He looked up, saw me peeking in the kitchen window and fired a kill shot at me, instead of putting one in his brain. Lucky for me, Stringer's aim is bad; he's better with bombs and landmines. He shot out the window but missed me by a good three inches.

"Bubba, where the hell did you put the Kong DVD? I saw you throwing it around last week like a frisbee."

I hate that movie. Why Stringer thinks I want to watch two hours of everyone shooting and bombing a big gorilla who is minding his own business is beyond me. I think he only watches it to make me upset. I took care of that. He won't find it. We're going out tonight. Let's see what kind of trouble we can get into at Roma's town meeting. Best show in town, well really, the only show in town.

After Stringer fired that shot at me, I took it as an invitation and climbed inside through the broken window. I was damn near frozen that night, so a bullet to the head would at least have warmed me up. Stringer just sat there, gun still locked and loaded, watching me jump around the room and then settle down in front of his fireplace. He stared at me for a long time. I just stared back at him like we were in a staring contest. Then everything from that horrible night caught up with me. I fell into a deep sleep and have lived here ever since.

"You know what, Bubba? I'm thinking maybe we should go out and pick up some food and beverages before it gets worse. If we're gonna get snowed in again for a few days, we really ought to have some provisions. I hear you. I know it was your idea. But it's me who's got to do the driving."

Stringer drives the plow truck around Roma. He plows everyone's driveways in the winter and makes pretty good money, just enough to get us through the rest of the year. He hates to drive unless he's plowing.

"Where's my fucking keys, Bubba? You wanna go out so bad then you find my keys, you crazy-ass monkey. My other boot too. Why do you keep on moving everything? Just leave my shit where I put it, Bubba."

Stringer says it was that one day in the Mekong Delta that changed everything for him. His platoon was heading back to base camp after being out in the jungle for six days straight. Stringer's job was to blow shit up, so that's what he'd been doing. But that day was the first time in four years he saw first-hand what damage he had caused. Walking back through the burned-out villages, he saw the dead bodies and witnessed the orphaned children sitting next to the scattered carcasses of their mothers and fathers. He remembers one little boy still holding the hand of his mother, not attached to anyone anymore. Three months later his second tour was up. He left Vietnam forever, a broken man with no joy for life or hope for the future at the ripe old age of twenty-four. I found him two years later with that .45 cocked, aimed and ready to end his painful existence.

"Found my boot, Bubba, right under your accordion where you put it. I mean why would you even touch my boot? It stinks and it's usually wet. You better not be pissing in it. I taught you how to use the toilet, Bubba. That's where monkeys go in this house, never in my boots."

Funny how that night I showed up outside Stringer's window turned out to be the night we both got saved. Just a couple of more minutes outside and I would have been one frozen Capuchin monkey. Just a few seconds later and Stringer would have had a back door opening to his big head. That night the universe had a better plan for the both of us.

"Now my keys, find my keys, Bubba, and we're outta here. Keys, Bubba, now..."

I always put Stringer's truck keys in the refrigerator fruit-and-vegetable drawer because he never ever looks in there, doesn't even use it. It's also the same place where I stash the Kong DVD. I hide his keys so he doesn't drive the plow over someone's house when he's been drinking. That would be one of those big stupid mistakes Stringer would never recover from. Stringer doesn't like people much, but he definitely doesn't want to hurt anyone else. He's all done with that.

"What is it with you and my keys, Bubba? You like them because they're shiny?"

Yeah, that's it, I'm all about the shiny. Who came up with monkeys like shiny things? Actually though, it was Stringer's shining lights that brought me to his window that freezing cold night. At four in the morning, his house was the only one with the lights still on. They were taking me to Montreal in a van that skidded off the highway, killing the driver and spewing fifty caged monkeys all along Exit 10. My cage broke open so I took off into the trees, like any monkey would. I jumped limb to limb for what seemed like a long time. Just when I was ready to let go and give into the big freeze, I could see a light shining through the trees. It was Stringer's lighthouse.

Funny, how just a week before I was living the warm and humid tropical life in Costa Rica. My days were spent playing in the trees, screeching at tourists and eating green bananas. Then, from out of nowhere, some scientist shoots me in the ass with a tranquilizer gun and I'm on my way to the Neuro Center in Montreal for experiments, which never end well for the monkeys.

"Move it, Bubba, let's make the store before Rufus closes up. We need some provisions to eat and drink our way through this storm. Gonna be too much snow to even plow tomorrow."

As we drive down the mountain road into the town of Roma, or what is left of it, Stringer points to the empty storefronts and abandoned buildings and recollects how wonderful everything used to be. Like everyone else still here, Stringer hangs onto Roma's glory days, the best days of his life, which came to a screeching halt far too early.

"Alright, Bubba, you wait here. I'll be just a few minutes in the store. You know how nervous Rufus gets when he sees you. He's probably gonna be at the town meeting too, so just leave him and everyone else alone. Hear me? I'm putting in The Monkey's 'Daydream Believer' for you, your favorite. Now keep your seatbelt on and just be cool. I'll be right back."

Oh, I'm cool alright. But that yard ornament gnome of a Rufus better stop eyeballing me like he's doing right now from his store window. I swear, he locks eyes with me in that town meeting even once and we're throwing it down. Because that's what monkeys do, we throw down. You don't need no science experiment to figure that out. Just come to Roma's town meeting tonight and see what happens.

**...L'Chaim Baby, L'Chaim...**
Childhood was all daydreams and play,
The teens just one long bad day;
My 20s was wild, My 30s much less,
Those 40s brought smiles, But 50s the best;
My 60s marched slowly into 70s forced calm,
Now these silent night 80s embrace me,
Whispering 'time to move on'.
Born to this moment let infant begin,
This journey called life,
Your own bumpy ride to our unfinished end.
**...To Life Baby, To Life...**


Chester Connelly
12th Grade Roma High School
Honorable Mention Poetry Contest

# DEATH OF THE HERETIC

Everyone who knew him even a little is here. We're all standing in a freezing rain, the kind that turns everything and everyone into glass statues, frozen in place soon as it hits. I can hear him laughing at us one last time, just like he always did...

Chester Connelly wasn't born in Roma, but his family moved here from Boston when he was just three years old, so we always thought of him as an original Romite, a townie. We all grew up together, playing in each other's backyards, then going to elementary, middle and high school as one family class. In any town, but most especially in a small town like Roma, that's a journey that bonds you forever. I knew him the longest so our connection was even stronger. We all had our moments with Chester, moments that stay with you. Some were strange, some were beautiful, but all of them unforgettable, maybe even profound. You might say he was one of a kind, a genuine piece of work. To me he was just Chester, the guy who saw and smelled bullshit from a mile away, laughing at the farce of it all, and at all of us for taking it so seriously.

Chester was a heretic in the purest sense of the word, and damn proud of it. He didn't stop at religion, though he loved arguing with Reverend Digby about church doctrine. No, Chester was an equal-opportunity heretic, attacking all areas of hypocrisy and nonsensical behavior so easy to find in and about Roma. Funny how today we all show up to bid him farewell, to wave goodbye and bon voyage to Chester Connelly, that guy who always pointed the finger, usually his middle one, when Roma wasn't acting real. Lately, that was a very busy finger.

At one time or another we all heard Chester's go-to line, "If it ain't real, it just don't matter." Me? Just by luck, I knew him first, before anyone else. Growing up we were always playing, running across everybody's backyard like it was just one continuous field for our endless kickball games. Chester was a legendary kickball player. His nickname back then was 'The Foot' because of how high and far he could kick the ball. He even wore a special steel-toed shoe for a while, just to protect his left kicking foot. Chester believed he was going to play kickball professionally until one day he found out there was no such thing. That was a devastating moment for Chester, as nobody told him until we reached high school and he showed up for tryouts.

I'm Roma's only limo driver, which gives me a monopoly on weddings, airports and on this miserable excuse of a Friday, funerals. They call me 'Wheels' because the only time anyone sees me around town is when I'm driving my long black limo. Other than that, I keep to myself.

Back in Roma's heyday, we used to have a whole fleet of fifteen sleek limos shuttling people back and forth to their ski vacations, parties and corporate events. Extramarital affairs were a big chunk of business too—they always hired a limo for privacy and always paid cash, usually in 'Hundys'. I still get a few of those from time to time, but Roma's just not the prime destination for romantic getaways like she used to be. Roma got tired and rundown these last few years. She needs a paint job, or as Chester liked to say, "...we need to put some lipstick on the pig."

I remember the town meeting just a few years back when Chester took it to our scary Mayor, Mary Yeldir, or as Chester liked to call her, Bloody Mary...

"If you can't even admit what's going on to the people who live here and care about Roma, well then Mayor Mary I believe it's clear that you've become blind, deaf and officially dumb. No, I'm going to keep talking. I waited my turn and like that old man who did those monkey movies once said, "I paid for this microphone." This town's dying. Too many young people and families are moving away. Any idiot can see it. We need to make some changes to attract more people here, instead of acting like everything's fine and dandy and we don't want any outsiders in Roma. Hell, outsiders are exactly who we do need—new blood, new energy, new ideas, new investment—or there will be no more Roma. We'll just become a gas stop and a convenience store on the way up the mountain to the ski slope, so long as that stays open."

Bloody Mary always stood up holding her gavel when she was responding to Chester. Our Mayor is an imposing woman who looks especially scary when she stands before you banging her hammer.

"Now, Chester, things aren't as dire as all that. Lots of other towns are seeing families move away, back to the big cities. That's where the jobs are. But none of these other towns have died out yet."

"YET—that's your keyword there, most Honorable Mayor–YET. 'Died out', that's wide open to interpretation. Let's take a quick look at the population declines— Umbraville, population five thousand just two years ago, today barely a thousand; Sienna Falls, nearly seven thousand people three years ago, today not even two thousand. Shall I go on? Trusca was nearly ten thousand solid citizens, now barely fifty-five hundred and falling as we speak. Wellsboro is down to just thirty-five hundred people from almost eight thousand in just three years. Are you noticing a trend here, Mayor Mary? I am. What I'm saying, is we can't just bury our heads in the sand and hope things will get better...you can't deal with a problem if you can't even admit you have one."

Yes, Chester had a way of getting under Mayor Mary's skin. Chester used to say, the only thing he really liked about Bloody Mary was the way she argued, how she never gave an inch even when she was completely wrong. She always went for the kill punch. Now, here she stands today, front row center. She's looking even scarier than usual, without even pounding her hammer, looking down at Chester's casket with mascara tears streaking her face, or maybe it's just the rain pellets. I guess Chester got to have the last word this time.

I see Reverend Digby scowling from beneath a big black umbrella as people file up one by one to drop flowers on Chester's casket. Reverend Digby was always Chester's favorite target. They never agreed on anything, especially about religion. Since Chester was not exactly what you'd call a churchgoer, they'd usually meet up at our general store to hold their debates...

"I tell you Reverend, if we just get rid of all the organized religions, especially yours, then most of what people argue about and kill each other over will be gone...all that'll be left to cause trouble are women and money, in that order."

"Chester, I don't even know where to begin with what you just said, but the reality is people, even you, no, especially you, Chester, need guidance toward how to live a good life."

"The Crucifixion, The Crusades, The Inquisition. The Reformation, The Holocaust...were these the guideposts for that good life, Reverend? As I see it, throughout history people were better off and enjoying their lives much more before all of this divine guidance reared its ugly head and started telling us how we should live our lives."

"You're just pulling out the negative events, Chester, and yes, I do agree there are more than a few. I don't proclaim to understand why these atrocities happened. But what about all the people, and there are many, who have found peace and hope in their chosen faith, in believing in God?"

"See now, that's where we agree Reverend Digby. It's not the church they attend, or what faith they label themselves that has anything to do with that peace and hope you talk about. No, these are the people who have made a choice to believe that there is a God, that there are reasons and some grand plan that explain all the ugly and horrible things that have already happened and keep on happening in this ridiculous Purgatory world we live in. Let's call them the True Believers. It doesn't much matter where they go to worship and pray, top of the mountain or middle of the ocean—a Jew can chant in a mosque, a Baptist sing hymns to the Vatican, or a Catholic pray the rosary in a Buddhist temple—they're all still going to believe in their very own understanding of God, right up until that moment when they just do or don't believe anymore, Reverend; right up until that final moment when they either keep or lose their hope and faith for things ever getting better."

Rufus Reardon, the General Store's owner, always tried to quickly end their fiery exchanges when other customers walked in.

"Excuse me, but are you two gonna buy anything, or are you just here to argue about God and the hereafter? I'm pretty sure God wants you to buy stuff when you come into my store."

I can see Rufus standing in the back of the crowd today, just like at the town meetings, standing next to Katie Konklin, his elementary school crush he never got over. Rufus looks like an old farmer from Scotland with his full grey beard and scraggly long hair. He could be one of those bearded characters from Brigadoon, the land that time forgot, which isn't too different a place from Roma. Katie, on the other hand, is a classic blond-haired, blue-eyed beauty, and much taller than Rufus. They make an odd couple, or would, if they ever were a couple.

Chester always loved talking to Rufus about why his business was failing. "I'm telling you, Rufus, it's not even your fault. Of course business is down. Nobody's got any money to pay for anything anymore. I'm surprised, even impressed you're still open at all. Your store's the same great store it's always been. It's Capitalism that's failed you, Ruf. It was never supposed to work for everyone, only for the Capitalists. That's the rich folk, Rufus, people with the capital, the money, the denaro. Adam Smith knew it from the beginning when he wrote about Greed, and how it was the only thing that could cause the downfall of his grand plan called, Capitalism. He never could have imagined what havoc technology would rain on Capitalism, with everyone losing their jobs because a computer can do it better, quicker, and of course, cheaper. Nope, Mr. Smith never saw that storm cloud coming.

"You think communism is a better way to go? Are you one of them there communists, Chester?"

"Nah, Communism doesn't work either. Same reason too, greed. Turns out we're all just a bunch of greedy bastards. Soon as people get into power, get themselves even just a little bit of control, they don't want to be communists anymore. They'd rather live large and party like Capitalists. No, Rufus, we've got to do it like Canada does, and Australia, Sweden and Iceland, all those smaller countries where people are living high-quality lives. We have to mix Capitalism with Socialism. I'm telling you, that's what they've done Rufus. It's the model that works for everyone, not for just a handful of rich white people who probably inherited their wealth anyway."

"Thing is Ruf, we're already doing Socialism here. We're propping up the banks, the stock market and the corporations with government money so they can keep living the good life. All I'm saying is, let's give that same government money and good life to everyone. That sounds fair huh, Rufus?"

"I hear what you're saying, Chester, but they're all much smaller countries. It's easier for them to take care of everyone. We're over three-hundred-thirty million people in the U.S., and that's not even counting the illegals. What we need are good jobs for people to make money, so they can go out and spend it. Until that happens, nothing's going to change. We'll just be a bunch of people with great healthcare and higher education standing around doing nothing, and still not making or spending any money. If Canada is doing so much better, you should go and live there, Chester. Send me a postcard."

"Nah, I'm an American. I like living in Roma where all my friends are. I just can't understand why we don't outlaw greed, spread the wealth and make life a good time for everyone, not just the lucky few. Turns out Capitalism is the biggest Ponzi scheme of all time. The people who got here first made a killing, mostly as robber barons and slave owners. The rest of us are just picking up their crumbs. You can see it in the stock and bond markets every day. It's just a pyramid scheme made legal, a rigged game for who?—for the Capitalists, Rufus. It's time to change the game, update the model; hell, Smith's Capitalism scheme is two-hundred and fifty years old now. Of course it's obsolete. The bible has been rewritten three times, at least; the Constitution amended twenty-seven times, and counting. But nobody's laid a hand or a glove on Capitalism, Rufus. Not a single one of those self-proclaimed geniuses on the TV has the balls to point their middle fingers at that greedy five-hundred pound gorilla sitting in the middle of the room, eating too many bananas and drinking all the champagne. They're all just a bunch of intellectual pussies, Rufus, afraid to say what needs to be said. Capitalism is the problem;  it needs to be updated to include everyone ."

Yeah, Chester had a way of getting under Rufus's skin too, especially because Chester dated Katie Konklin for a while back in high school. Of course, Chester dated just about every girl in town for a while. Most of them are here today, even though they're not single anymore. I always loved listening to Chester chatting up the girls. Nobody had a better line of charm than Chester. He used to say, "It's all about the communication boys. That's all they really want. Make them laugh, even just a little bit and that'll take you a long way into the night."

Rain's falling down even harder now. Ice pellets feel like tiny frozen daggers as they hit my face, and all the faces here today, lost in remembering Chester Connelly. We're all forced to lower our heads as if in homage to a great man, but really it's to save face from the storm's battering. Yeah, that's Chester I hear, roaring with laughter from behind his big toothy grin. He's relishing this torturous moment for us all.

Funny thing about Chester, pain in the ass that he was, he really cared about, even enjoyed most people. When you spoke with him he listened, truly heard you. Then he'd respond with what he called 'Chester Wisdom', usually the opposite of conventional. The trick to a happy life according to Chester was never to become a cliche. "Don't ever let 'em label you." That's a funny thing to say to a man nicknamed 'Wheels'.

Heroin addicts, alcoholics, criminals, sex addicts, bullies and all the rest...according to Chester, anyone who becomes addicted to a certain type of behavior or dependent on any one thing has become a simple cliché in life — predictable and boring. They'd given in and let society label them.

I was with Chester the day it happened, on that last round of golf he ever played. Nobody would have labeled him one, but Chester was a passionate golfer. He loved to play the game, said he felt very Zen walking the course trying to hit the tiny ball into the tiny hole hundreds of yards away. He wasn't a very good golfer, rarely breaking a hundred on his scorecard, and that was with a fair amount of creative accounting in adding up his strokes. His method was to divide the number of putts he took by two, and he'd never count his mishits when teeing off. Not very PGA. It was always a special day when Chester broke one hundred, or a 'Hundy', as Chester liked to call it.

"I've never seen an ugly course, Wheels. That's why I like to walk when I play. They're always green and serene. No better place to take a relaxing walk and get deep inside the head. No cart for me. It's the walking that makes you feel alive and awake out here. Those cart guys, they're missing out. Now, if I could just get that damn ball to cooperate."

It was last week, late October, when Chester played his final round. The course was already closed for the season. All the grounds crew had gone home for their long winter naps. Flags had been taken down from the greens, and leaves were blowing everywhere, covering the fairways and making it almost impossible to track your ball. Even on beautiful sunny days, Chester always had a hard time finding his ball. He dropped many, usually in the middle of the fairway for a better shot than from behind the trees where his ball had a habit of landing, and then disappearing.

But this was a stormy, windy day with an early October snow forecast. It was one of those days that just couldn't make up its mind between fall and winter. Just when we thought the sun might break through, the wind would kick up and it would start to rain, even thunder a bit off in the distance. Then a little snow mixed in with the rain, and I thought maybe we should call it a day as we were just hitting the back nine. Chester would hear none of it though. He wasn't ready to quit.

"Are you kidding me, Wheels? I'm having my best round ever. Without even fudging, I'm just three over par."

He was actually six over par, but he was right, this was by far Chester's best round of golf, ever. Too bad I was the only witness to the magic that happened on Chester's last nine holes that afternoon. That's really the beauty of golf, the thing people who don't play don't understand. On any given day, on any given course, anyone can play above themselves, play like a pro. They can reach levels of performance they've never achieved before. Chester had that day. He lived that Zen moment he had been searching for, and then he moved on.

Helped by the wind, he was hitting his tee shots 280 to 320 yards, and they were flying straight down the fairway. Chester always did hit the ball hard and long, it just rarely went straight. Usually, it was hard right or hard left. His favorite call was to yell "Fore" just before he teed off to warn any nearby golfers about the ball that was potentially going to hit them on their noggin in the next few seconds. More than a few times he saved them from the concussion.

The worst part of Chester's game, and there were many to choose from, but his true nightmare shot was the medium range, from fifty to one hundred yards off the green. This was usually when Chester would launch the ball smoothly into the air, driving it at least two hundred yards into the woods, or at somebody's passing cart on an adjacent hole.

On this strange windy day there was no reason to yell "Fore" as we were the only ones on the course. Also, Chester was landing his drives not only on the green but surprisingly close to the hole. If I hadn't witnessed it myself, I never would have believed him. But there it was, Chester was dominating the back nine. He was one-putting the greens, sinking putts from fifteen feet away like they were 'gimmes'. As another one dropped into the cup, Chester said, "It's all in the backspin, Wheels, all about that backspin."

By the eighteenth hole, Chester's scorecard was at thirty for the back eight, with just one to go. He was playing even better with each swing and was truly four shots under par. The wind was gusting by this time. I wanted to get eighteen over with and back to the car, but Chester was talking about playing the first nine holes over again. He just didn't want this day to end, this feeling to go away. I understood, but I also could see the dark clouds coming, and moving in fast. It was time to go home.

Thunder rolled and lightning flashed just over the mountains as Chester crushed his tee shot on eighteen. It was a beautiful ball, a rising line drive so pure and true I thought it might never land at all, just keep soaring past the clubhouse and beyond the parking lot. But land it did, bouncing on the front lip of the green then skimming along the wet grass all the way to the tin cup. There it sat, just inches away, waiting for the tap in. Chester sang, 'O Danny Boy, as the rain poured down and we walked the last three-hundred-twenty-five yards to his final green.

By the time we reached the eighteenth hole, the wind had pumped up to what felt like fifty miles an hour. I told Chester to pick up the ball and get us out of here. He just laughed, pulled out his putter and lined up his twelve-inch putt. But he never got the chance to make that putt. The wind did it for him, blowing across the green at just the right angle, guiding Chester's ball gently into the cup, giving him a hole-in-one for the eighteenth and a thirty-one for the back nine. Nobody was ever going to believe this ever happened. I didn't care, I witnessed it live and in person. Chester reached into the cup, turned and raised his putter up in the air as he did his Irish victory jig around the hole. By now, the windstorm had turned violent, capped by rolling thunder, driving rain and squalling snow, to bring the imperfect storm upon us. But as Mark Twain once said between bourbon sips, as he waited out a violent storm on a Mississippi riverboat bound for St. Louis, "Thunder is good, Thunder is impressive, but it is Lightning that does the work." Mr. Twain could not have been more correct. Out of nowhere, a lightning bolt reached down from the heavens just as Chester raised his putter in victory to celebrate his unlikely hole-in-one.

Like a puppet on a string, Chester was pulled thirty feet up and away into the sky. The lightning lit him up like that Rockefeller Center Christmas tree, setting his hair on fire then dropping him back down to the green like a piece of burnt toast, landing him on top of the tin cup for another hole-in-one.

But it was the second bolt that really did the job, put the proverbial nail in his coffin. Just as Chester was sitting up, still holding his putter in the air with one hand and his ball in the other, another lightning bolt struck, making a direct hit on Chester's heart, ending what had been his best day ever.

They say getting hit by lightning even once is a one in a million chance. It's one in five million to get struck twice and if you do get struck, there's only a ten per cent chance of dying. Well Chester Connelly blew those odds away and then some. As I watched him sitting lifeless, smoldering and still smiling atop the tin cup at eighteen, I thought, 'He died with his putter in his hand, really not such a bad way to go'.

Looking around now, I see all of Chester's friends and neighbors who came to say farewell, or maybe just to make sure he was really dead. I see them running to their cars. This rainstorm we've all been standing in can now officially be classified as a deluge, and I know it's not going to end any time soon. It's just the beginning of what I am sure is going to be a long, very cold winter. Oh, how I can hear Chester roaring with laughter now.

As I walk to the empty limo waiting to take me home to my own deep sleep, I stop to look at the gravestone sitting on its side, ready to be placed. It's just a simple white stone monument saying all you really need to know about the man, whether you knew Chester or not, and I knew him very well...

**Here Rests Chester "Wheels" Connelly**
**Born October 24th, 1980**
**Died October 24th, 2020**
**"Make Mine A Double, And Hold All That Bullshit"**

## SHE WAS A SIMPLE MAN

I knew her then, I knew her when
The milk was all we had;
We played all day then touched all night,
Her whispers drove me mad;

She grew up fast, She came out strong,
Her teachers were all men;
But one by one she broke them all,
Their power in her hands;

Three senators, That general,
She only drank the best;
With each long sip these monsters knew,
She'd never let them rest;

She played their games but changed the rules,
Man's weakness was her strength;
But in the end each played her fool,
Left helpless in her wake;

Me? I've watched her all these years,
Her private confidante;
We share a name but wear no shame,
Her love is all I want;

I'll wait for her, She always comes,
She can't forget her first;
We tell a secret most would shun,
Her body tames my thirst; Together, Forever we are cursed.
**Roscoe Ridley — Arriving in Roma**

## SHE WAS A SIMPLE MAN

"Yes, Mary, I will pick you up at two-thirty. I promise not to be late."

Nobody really understands Mayor Mary the way I do. How could they?

"At the church, what are you doing at the church? Alright, I'll be there. Yes, I'll leave my cell phone on, just like always. See you soon, Mary, I mean Mayor."

I know she comes off as scary to some people, probably most, alright to everyone. But behind that aggressive exterior is a woman out to change the world. Mary's got her very own view of how things should be, and she's always had the power to back it up. Hell, she's six feet tall, a hundred and eighty pounds, built like a linebacker with formidable breasts who likes to tackle hard. Why would anyone want to get in her way?

To put it simply, Mayor Mary believes men, all men including me, are simple-minded idiots. As a group, we're a bunch of fuck-ups who have messed everything up and ruined the world we now live in. She blames all the world's problems, all of our country's problems, which have become all of Roma's problems, on the men in positions of power who made foolish decisions and horrible choices based mainly on greed and ego. If the men in charge had seen what was happening early-on and had the balls to do something about it, then Roma would still be a thriving town today instead of the forgotten rundown has-been resort it has become.

According to Mayor Mary, men have no balls, no real balls. It's women who are far superior, and the only chance our world has for survival is for the women to take control of everything. "The world needs nurturing, and men are ill-equipped to do it," Mary always says. Men just keep fucking things up and then wonder why everything is so fucked up. I've heard it so many times over the years. I guess you could say I'm an authority on Mayor Mary. I've known her since we were kids, even before. I've watched her take on and break down one blowhard after another. In the end, when Mary was all done with them, it was always her on top in complete control and them asking for permission to use the bathroom.

Mary says men are innately weak. The more powerful we act, the weaker we are on the inside. All she does is help the man find and embrace his inner weakness. The rest is easy. Once Mary or any woman takes control, the man can never recover his power because it was never real to begin with. It was just a hollow birthright. The true power always did belong to the woman, to Mary and all the other Marys of this world.

She just doesn't get why a woman would choose to be weak when they are naturally filled with so much power over men. It shows in most relationships where it's the woman who is truly in charge. She's the real boss behind the scenes, while the silly man masquerades in public as the king of the hill...

"Chief, it's Rufus."

"I know Rufus. Your name pops up on my phone, every time you call."

"Just wanted to let you know the fires from last night are still burning up there off Mountain Road."

"Yeah, Rufus, I can see the smoke. We did everything we could to contain them, but they just won't burn out. Peculiar fires, they won't douse no matter what we use on them. Anyway, I'll ask Chief Satchmo to check them out later. Anything else, Rufus?"

"I don't see why you don't just lock up Billy and his cohorts to put an end to these fires. They're getting closer to the town."

"You know why, Rufus. Because we never can catch them doing it, and Billy swears he's not starting them. Have to go now, Rufus."

"Oh yeah, Henry Huntington's in town..."

"Saw your posting on the gossip blog. Thanks for the heads up."

Rufus calls me almost as much as Mayor Mary does. His heart's in the right place when it comes to Roma. He just doesn't always have his facts straight. I remember his first suspect for starting these fires was Bubba, Stringer's monkey. Rufus hates Bubba. It took a while but now Rufus accepts that Bubba has an airtight alibi; he's always with Stringer, and Stringer's always home. So now Billy's his prime suspect. Mine too.

Mary and me, we didn't grow up in Roma like most of the folks did who still live here. No, we moved to Roma about ten years ago when Roma was still Roma. Mary arrived first, like she always does. I came a couple of minutes, I mean months later. We moved to Roma from Washington D.C., where Mary stayed busy as a lobbyist showing the generals and senators who was really in charge. It never ceases to amaze me how Mary always picks out the biggest, meanest, ugliest bullies in the schoolyard and turns them into her very own needy little lap dogs without even breaking a sweat. Nobody does that better than Mary, though according to her all women could and should.

"The world would be a much better place to live if women were in charge of everything," Mary says. "Even on your very best days men are morons, and you just barely make that low bar of performance." Mary's hard on men.

Who's that up ahead? "Hello, Samantha. Out and about today are you? Just want to let you know it's kind of hard to see you coming around the bend here. With the road icing up like it is, maybe you should move further back while you play your fiddle. Storm's getting worse, it might be a good time to get on home now. I'd give you a ride but I'm heading all the way up the mountain first."

"Thanks, Chief Ridley, we'll be careful. Just a few more songs with my band and we'll head home. We just sound so much better outside with the snow blowing through the trees giving us the natural acoustic setting."

Poor kid, she hasn't had her family band since the accidents took them all a few years back. "You know I stopped by your place, your family home over the holidays. People called in saying they kept seeing lights going on and off up there. But when I checked it out, the place looked dark to me. So much snow, I couldn't even see in the windows. Were you up there Samantha?"

"I was home for a while, Chief, just cleaning up and getting things ready for the holidays. Must have been me they saw."

Getting ready for what? Samantha's got no family, she's the only Strange left. "That's probably it, I must have just missed you. Be safe, Samantha. Stay well off the road and don't be out too late. This storm's going to be another humdinger. Now play one for me as I drive off into the sunset. Let's pretend there is a sunset." *'Waltzing Matilda'* fills the silence as the snow falls and the ice gathers around Samantha and her invisible band.

"It was him. Those lights I saw outside, it was Chief Ridley," Samantha whispers to her Strange Family Band.

It's her house, they left it to her. Can't tell the kid she's not allowed up there. Just wish she had more adult supervision, with her family all deceased like that. She's staying with the Harrisons, a good family. But they never know where she's at, playing her fiddle all over town like she does. Strange kid that Samantha. Roma just wouldn't be the same without Samantha and her fiddle playing.

"Yes, Mary, I saw the Rufus posting too. I know Henry's in town. I'm heading up the mountain road right now. I'll catch up with Henry and send him your way. Yes, I promise to be more assertive with him this time. I'll see you soon, Mayor Mary...yes, two-thirty at the church, I remember. You at a church, how could I forget."

I've got to say, Mary's been acting stranger than usual lately. What the hell is she doing at the church? She usually stays as far away from religion as she can. She seems in a hurry lately too, like time's running out or she's on a deadline for something. That usually means she's getting ready to move on, time to relocate. She hasn't said anything to me, but she never does. Just packs her bags and disappears into the night, leaving me to clean up her mess, which I never can. Then I follow along behind her.

From when we were kids, and even before, Mary's been the leader and me her loyal follower. Mary's that force of nature who can go anywhere, size up the people and take control of the situation. Over the years, I've watched her dethrone the kings and behead the monsters. I have to say, every one of those horrible men deserved what they got from Mary Yeldir. But me, I'm different. We're connected forever. I have no choice but to follow her all the way to our journey's end. Her fight is my fight too. When Mary's all done with Roma, so am I. Wherever she goes, I'll find her. Because twins, especially us younger ones, we're loyal like that.

## PITY THE POOR TRUST FUNDER

Seems like no matter how many times I leave Roma I keep getting sucked back into this black hole of a town that eats up everything and everyone coming anywhere near it. I can't believe our place hasn't sold yet. Problem is, the house is just too fucking big. Rich people used to like showing off how much money they had by building ridiculously oversized mansions. Now it's the opposite. These days, people with serious money go small so they can stay anonymous and have plenty of cash on hand for the Armageddon.

Trying to sell a mansion today is like playing Old Maid—who's going to get stuck with it. I just don't get why people still live out here surrounded by mountains in the middle of nowhere. Hell, even the realtors have left town. That's when you know the jig is up, when the cheerleaders stop cheering about how great Roma is. Now it's just a bunch of For Sale by Owner signs. I get to drive all the way up from Boston to show our mansion on the hill to looky-looks who have no real intention of actually buying it, even at twenty-five cents on the dollar. Who is that waving at me up ahead? Oh, it's Chief-Fucking-Ridley. Every time I come to town he pops up out of nowhere and feels the need to talk to me. I just don't want this today. Next time, if there is one, I'm coming after dark. I mean, what does he even do these days? Roma doesn't need a police force, there's nothing left to steal. I'm pretty sure the Chief and Mayor Mary are screwing the town blue, when they're not doing whatever it is they do to each other.

"Hello again, Chief Ridley. I'm back. As always, it's good to see you."

"Good afternoon, Henry. Rufus put it up on the Porch Chat that you were back in town." Rufus, that fuckin asshole. That's how Chief Ridley always knows I'm here. Rufus posts it on the Roma gossip site.

"Yeah, that Rufus, Roma's very own town crier. He doesn't miss a trick. I'm showing the manor this afternoon to a couple from Boston, patrons of the museum."

"Good to hear, hope it sells. Such a waste, a beautiful home like yours sitting there empty all these years. It must cost a small fortune just to keep the heat and lights on. Speaking of money, Mayor Mary asked if you could stop by City Hall and say hello to her before you head back to Boston. There's still that matter of back taxes she wants to clear up."

"Yes, I know, Chief. In fact, I'm painfully aware. I did tell my mother the last time, and the time before that. She was going to send a check. Didn't get one yet? It must still be in the mail. I'll stop by today, always a pleasure to chat with Mayor Mary."

"You're one of the few who says that with a straight face Henry. She's a tough nut. Believe me, I know. Another blizzard coming tonight, don't be on the road too late."

"Thanks, Chief. I should be leaving around three unless they actually want to buy the place. Then I'll stick around until the deal is done, could be a couple of days. There's so much snow this year, too much to even ski."

"Yeah Henry, it's been one long cold winter. We got our first snow in August this year—August! It was just a summer dusting, but still. No sign of letting up either. Drive careful, the roads are already slick. Good luck with the manor and make some time for the Mayor."

"Sure will, Chief. See You..."

"Like hell I will. That woman has anger issues. I'm positive she's killed people. We'll pay the taxes when we sell the fucking house, if we have anything left over. Don't know what Dad was thinking building such a monstrosity. But that's what you did back then huh, Dad, show who had the biggest dick by square footage."

"No, Henry, that's what we did as a testament to our success. Your great-grandfather built it, my father added on to it, and I made it even bigger. Do you see a pattern here son? Now you're going to sell it. Makes me want to weep, Henry."

"It looks like a spaceship that landed on the wrong planet, Dad. Mother and me, we both live in Boston now. I hardly ever get up here. I come as rarely as possible in fact. Roma's become a real shithole."

"The town has gone downhill, I'll give you that. But the mountain, the forests, the valleys, they're all still beautiful. That was why we built here, Henry. It was always about the land, never the town. People come, and people go, but the land stays forever. You can always count on the land to save you, Henry."

"Well if I can't sell the manor soon, I'm thinking of setting a bonfire to collect on the insurance before we stop paying it. At this point, we'll make more money on the settlement than from any sale. Nobody can afford to buy it. The developers want to knock it down to build condos, and they don't want to pay hardly anything for it. If I can cut a deal for fifty cents on the dollar, you should be proud of me."

·

"I'm not going to be proud of you for burning down the house your great-granddad built with his bare hands. It's Huntington Manor for God sake, your legacy Henry, show some respect."

"Will you look at that? It's Little Ivan walking down the mountain in this snowstorm. It must be his day off from the museum because he never leaves that place. Crazy little dude, hates my guts. I can tell just by the way he looks at me, like he wants to spit on the ground every time I walk by. I'd fire him tomorrow if we didn't need him so bad. He's the only one who knows how to work all those security cameras. Fuckin little know-it-all. I'm gonna give him a honk just to let him know it's me driving by. Was that the middle finger? Did Little Ivan give me the fuck-you finger? You know what? Fuck him. I'm gonna fire that little bastard just as soon as I get back to Boston. To hell with security, I should have done it a long time ago."

"Ah, there she blows, Huntington Manor in all her glory. I wish you and your mother would move back here so we could all be a family again."

"Problem is, you're dead, Dad. We're not exactly a normal family anymore. I don't think we ever really were. We were more like those crazy royals who came to Roma to play and recreate. We never actually made any friends here, you know."

"Funny, I seem to remember so many good days here with you. Skiing, hiking, hunting, fishing, riding bikes and horses...we did it all. Our quality time in the wilderness happened here, bonding father and son forever, 'recreating' as you like to say.  Who talks like that? You've been spending way too much time with your mother, the woman who refuses to venture into the great outdoors, or even her own backyard. She's turned you into a namby-pamby city dweller, Henry."

"Nobody who matters lives in the country anymore Dad, we visit. Look at Roma. The only people still here are the ones who can't leave. They're trapped. They have no place else to go. Times have changed. There's really no good reason to leave the city anymore. You can have life delivered to your front door, even to your couch if you're too lazy to get up."

"What has she done to you? This can't be my son talking. You're Henry Huntington for God sake, a chip off the old block—my block, and my father's block and his father's block before him. You're a blue-blood, a true American, so start acting like it. There's just no way in hell you're going to sell our family retreat for pennies on the dollar. Not today, not tomorrow, not while I'm still around."

"That's just it, Dad, you're not still around. Only to me, and I really wish that would stop. I'm hoping that when I sell the manor you go along with it, like a package deal."

"That's not the way it works, Henry. Oh my God, is that them? They've got 'Bed and Breakfast' written all over them. Are they Poofters?"

"Hello. Hope you haven't been waiting too long. It was slow-going up the mountain road. I'm Henry Huntington and welcome to Huntington Manor."

"Hello, Henry. I'm Tucker and this is Rolley. It's even more grandiose than in the photos. How many square feet?"

"I don't like them already. How many square feet? Is that all that matters? What about all the detailed woodwork? They've never seen woodwork like this in their lives."

"It's just over forty-thousand square feet of living space with ten bedrooms, ten bathrooms and ten working fireplaces. When I was growing up, we called it our country getaway, our family camp."

"Did you have a large family Henry?"

"You might think so but no, Rolley. It was just my dad, my mother and me. My mother always hated the country, so it was mostly my dad and me and lots of weekend guests. Dad loved to entertain. This was quite the party house back in the seventies and eighties."

"Well we love the place, Henry, it's very special. We see it as a spa for city dwellers who want to rejuvenate and escape the chaos.

"I knew it. These lily-dippers want to turn it into a spa. That's even worse than a Bed and Breakfast...it's Sodom and Gomorrah, with scented towels and avocado water. Not happening on my watch, not while I'm still alive and kicking."

"Again, Dad, you're not."

"What did you say, Henry?"

"Oh, I'm sorry, Tucker. Sometimes I respond to the voices in my head. Hell, really it's just one voice, my dad's, who of course is long dead. He just refuses to admit it."

"Wow, really? With me it's my mom; never shuts up and still always telling me how wrong I am about everything. She's been dead seven years now, and she's never been louder or more disapproving. Rolley talks to both his parents in his sleep, very spooky in the middle of the night."

"Just because they die doesn't mean they go away. I like it though, I miss them. Every night, usually around three in the morning they come into my dreams and tell me stories that I've mostly forgotten from when I was a kid. Then we go

142

for a walk and a picnic, very tranquil. They always put me into a deeper sleep. Tucker says I talk to them for about five minutes and then fall completely silent, like I'm not even breathing. The first few times he thought I had died, so he put the mirror up to my nose to make sure I was still breathing. I was. I like it though, knowing I'm going to see them and laugh with them on most nights. The nights they don't show up, I really don't sleep very well."

"Okay, this one I like. What's his name, Rawlsey? He can stay, but his buddy boy has got to go."

"We know all about the voices, Henry. Tell your dad he's welcome to stay if we end up buying this magical kingdom of yours. We promise to take good care of the place and restore her to the beauty she once was. We do believe in the power of rejuvenation, Henry, and we just love all the amazing woodwork throughout the house. So detailed."

"Tucker's starting to grow on me too."

"We've already taken the virtual tour, we've seen the photos and we did a walk-through with your broker, or your ex-broker now. Henry, we're here today to make you an offer."

"Up the price, Henry, up the price."

"Your asking price of twenty-five million is a bit higher than we want to go."

"Here it comes, Henry, the ten cents on the dollar offer. I knew these daffodils weren't for real the minute I saw them. What can I do to scare them off? I'm going to set their car on fire. Yes, that will do it. Step away, son."

"Henry, we love the seclusion of the place. Rolley even loves it that Roma's in need of a fresh coat of paint. We

143

see all sorts of business opportunities here. We'd like to offer you..."

"You're not taking a penny under fifteen million son, or I swear I will terrorize everyone who sets foot in here."

"...Twenty-one million for the land and everything on it, including of course Huntington Manor."

"Take it, Henry. Have them sign something right now. Do it before they change their minds."

"Rolley, Tucker, I think we can shake hands on this deal. Even my Dad sounds happy. Remember, he comes with the house. Good luck with that."

"Tucker and I wouldn't have it any other way. You're always welcome too, Henry. How about we meet in town and sign some papers over a bottle of wine? Our lawyers can work out the details."

"Wham-Bam...these guys sure do work fast. They've probably got the cash in a suitcase in their trunk. Close this deal, Henry."

"Grady's is the place, really the only place left standing. They still have a pretty good wine list. How about I meet you there in twenty minutes? Just be careful driving down that mountain road. It was already glazing over on my drive up here. Tucker, Rolley I seriously could not be happier that it's you two who are the new owners of Huntington Manor. Our family lodge couldn't be in better hands."

"Thank You, Henry. See you at Grady's. We'll open a bottle of red and let it breathe. But not for too long, so hurry up. Come on, Tucker. I'm freezing, and I'm driving."

"GTM Henry, GTM."

"I know, Dad, Get The Money. Your bottom-line take on the entire capitalist system...GTM, to hell with everyone and everything else. Well today, Dad, we finally do Get The Money, pay our  taxes and get the hell out of Roma, for good. We'll have some money back in this family again, at least for a little while."

"I'm wondering, why are they so hot to close this deal? Maybe there's oil or natural gas under our land. They look like frackers, Henry. Do not sell them the mineral rights."

"Please stop talking, Dad. In case you didn't notice it's coming down heavy now. I can barely see ten feet ahead of me and this car's just not made for mountain blizzard conditions. The road's just one long stretch of ice now. They get everything in the deal— the house, the land, the lake, and hopefully, you too since you seem to love it up here so much. You know what? I think I'm actually going to miss you, Dad. Not a lot, just a little bit. HOLY SHIT!  WHAT THE FUCK?"

"Hold on Henry, you're in a skid. I think you're supposed to steer into it, not away from it, son. Take your foot off the brake and just go with it. No, not like that. For God's sake don't give it the gas."

"I have no control, Dad. We're going sideways. What's that up ahead, some kid playing the violin in the middle of the road.  I think I'm going to hit her."

"That's the Strange kid, Samantha. Nice family. She shows up everywhere playing that fiddle. Don't worry son, you won't hit her, she's protected. Besides, we're skidding the other way. Look, she's waving at us."

"Here we go...I can't hold it, we're going over the side. Do you see that?  Some guy in a soldier uniform saluting us."

"You can see him? Well that explains a lot. Don't worry Henry, everything's going to be alright. If you can see

Sergeant Bruno that means you and me are going to be spending some quality father-son time together again. Hold my hand, Henry, just like when you were little. Relax and take a deep breath. I'll be right here with you son, the whole way over. I'm always with you, Henry."

"We're fuckin airborne. That's at least a hundred-foot drop. I can't believe this. Damn it, I finally sold the house. What about the twenty-one mill?"

"As usual, your mother will get the money, Henry. She taught me about GTM; she may have even invented the concept. I'm sure Tiger and Rawlsey will track her down in Boston to seal the deal. Good news is, Henry, you're not going to feel a thing. Now let's get this over with. Just hold on tight and we'll get back to the house and get you settled in. We've got some catching-up to do, son. I have so much to show you."

"I love you Dad. Always have."

"I know Henry, I know."

# THOU SHALT NOT...

"Bless me Father for I have sinned."

"How long has it been since your last confession, Mayor Mary?"

"At what age do we make our first confession, Reverend Digby?

"Usually just before you take your first communion, around age six or seven."

"I'm fiftyish now, so let's say it's been forty something years since my last confession. Possibly a little bit longer. But that's why I'm here today, Reverend Digby. I figured it was high time. So how does this confession forgiveness work, I've pretty much forgotten."

"It's really straightforward, Mary. You tell me your sins, the sins you believe you've committed and are sorry for, and I assign you some penance to absolve you from your sins."

"Then I'm all clean again, just like that? Isn't that what got the church into trouble way back when and started the whole Reformation thing? Do you still charge for the absolution, Reverend?"

"No, Mary, we don't charge anymore. People got upset about paying for their Indulgences, so now it's all free. Just be honest and tell me what sins you believe you may have committed against God and neighbor."

"Well, right off the bat, I know I've broken that first commandment about not worshipping any other gods. I started out as a Catholic just barely surviving my first eight years in school with the nuns, then went Hindu for a while during my college years. In my thirties, I got duped into Scientology until I saw how much money that was costing me. Then I switched into Yoga to reclaim my mind and body, which naturally led me to Buddhism, which is what I am these days whenever I'm feeling even slightly spiritual. But yes, I believe I have definitely worshipped at the feet of other gods, or at least we dated for a while."

"Well, Mary, I believe many people have probably broken that commandment as they try to figure out what works best for them in this world."

"So, are you saying I get a pass on that one Reverend, even though it's a commandment, the very first one? If you're giving out passes on this square, I'll take one."

"Well, not necessarily a pass, Mary, but let's just say you're in good company, or at least plenty of company here."

"Alright, Reverend Digby. I'm feeling a little bit better already. Now as far as number two goes, I have definitely taken the Lord's name in vain...probably twenty times...a day...for forty years…maybe fifty. But seriously, Reverend, who doesn't?"

"Again, Mary, many people have also broken this commandment. Is it a sin? Technically yes. Try not to do it anymore."

"I will, Reverend Digby, I promise I will. So far, I'm okay then. Not perfect but who is?"

"Let's just say, you're within the norm. Is that it, Mary?"

"Don't I wish...No, Reverend Digby, I'm just getting warmed up. I notice God started Moses off with the easy commandments, the misdemeanors, then turned up the heat to felonies on the second half of the tablets. Concerning number three, I haven't really kept the Sabbath, or any other holy day, if that means not drinking or having sex. No, as a rule, I usually stay pretty busy on Sundays, seeing how it's the last day and night of the weekend."

"As far as number four goes, honoring my father and my mother, well they were pretty much schmucks. They treated both me and my brother like shit, so I never really had any inclination to honor them. I did feel like killing them most of the time, but to my credit, I never did...kill them that is."

"I didn't know you had a brother, Mary. Are you two close?"

"We'll circle back to that one, Reverend, depending on how the rest of this goes. I'm pretty sure those third and fourth commandments are going to deliver me some fairly serious penance as I didn't just break them, I shattered them into little pieces."

"Let's skip commandment number five for now, the one about not killing anyone because I know that's a biggie. It's number six, Thou Shalt Not Commit Adultery...this one I'm guilty of sure, but guilty with an explanation, your honor."

"This one's pretty significant, Mary. Have you had sex with a married man? If your answer is yes, then you have committed adultery, a very serious sin against God and your neighbor."

"But it's really not that simple, Reverend Digby, and they were not my neighbors, though they did live close by. Now, you have to understand, there are happily married men and women and there are unhappily married men and women. It's the unhappy ones who will do anything, and I do mean anything, just to feel sexual again. Is it the marriage license that matters most here? I believe I have never had sex with a happily married man or woman and I should therefore receive a pass on this one as well...maybe one of those Indulgences you mentioned, free of charge of course so the Protestants don't get all upset again and start torturing people and cutting off their heads."

"No, that's a big one, Mary. You are not in good company here, as so many people get hurt when it comes to adultery. Was it just the one time?"

"Just the one time...no. It was definitely more than just the once, but, Reverend Digby, I'm no spring chicken. Also, it was them begging me for it by the time we actually had the sex. If I had to guess at a number, including both men and women plus a couple of transgenders, without being judged, Reverend, I'd round it off at about twenty-five times, give or take."

"Seriously Mary? I need a moment here. I'm having shortness of breath...Mary, that's a serious crime against God, and humanity in general. You are a serial adulterer. I'm not sure there even is a penance I can give that will forgive what you have done, Mary."

"I know, Reverend, I know. It's a lot to take in. Those bottom five are real killers. But I'm being totally honest here with you, not holding anything back. I want to come clean with everything so I can leave here with a clear conscience. Reverend Digby?"

"I'm in complete shock, Mary. I can't feel my legs. My entire lower body is numb, and I can only take short breaths through my mouth. I think I'm having a panic attack. You're only on number six and you skipped number five. I think we better stop here so I can get to the hospital."

"That's not fair to me, is it, Reverend? Aren't you supposed to hear all my sins before we adjourn this confession? Suck it up. Besides, I promised we'd come back to number five. It's the seventh one, Thou Shalt Not Steal, that I'm a little confused about. I need you to shed some light on this one for me. Of course I've stolen, everyone steals at some point in their lives. Whether it's those apples from the supermarket, earrings from the boutique, or maybe six hundred thousand dollars from the town budget—everyone steals. So long as nobody gets hurt in the process, I believe God understands. Like they say Reverend Digby, it's only money. God didn't invent money, man did. Here, I believe God is talking about stealing goats and rams and camels, mostly livestock. I've never done that. So I think I'm alright on number seven...Reverend?"

"You took money from the town budget? That's not only breaking a commandment, Mary, that's committing a criminal act, one that could put you in jail for a very long time. I feel nauseous. There's a ringing in my ears."

"But isn't there a privacy guarantee, that gag order covering everything that I tell you in the confessional remains confidential? All of this is a secret conversation between you, me and God, right, Reverend Digby?"

"Sadly yes, Mayor Mary, there is the sanctity of your confession, but..."

"No buts about it, Reverend Digby. I can either trust in you and God and the promises you make or I can't, and then the whole thing is a farce...just one giant waste of time. Can I trust you, Reverend?"

"Yes, Mayor Mary, you can trust me. I will never reveal to anyone what you have told me in your confession today. But your own conscience might force you to turn yourself in and right the wrongs you have done. Ultimately, it's your own forgiveness that matters the most."

"Don't you worry about me, Reverend, my conscience is just fine. My journey in life is always toward the greater good, making things better for women and the world in general. I'm fighting the good fight, Reverend Digby, and I'm winning. Just let me finish up here and assign me some of that penance so I can get on with things that need doing. Chief Ridley is picking me up soon. I've got to get back to the office for a meeting with Henry Huntington and collect those back taxes his family owes."

"I'm getting a really bad headache, it feels like an aneurism. The more you talk, Mary, the worse it gets. Please stop talking. I need to lie down and try to forget about all that you've told me here today. I really don't think there is a penance for all of these sins."

"Oh, Reverend, come on, God's forgiven worse than me. Let's finish up, we're almost there. Eight, nine and ten are sort of related anyway...they're all about Thy Neighbor. Sure, I have borne false witness, told lies about my neighbors— but only after they told lies about me first. The only way to fight a liar is to tell a juicier lie, put them on the defensive.

"I'm seeing spots, floating spots. Mary, you've got to stop, I need to pray. My throat is so dry. Please get me some water, I feel dehydrated..."

"As far as number nine goes, lusting after thy neighbor's wife and I assume husband, well who doesn't if their neighbor is good looking, or desirable in any way. I've had plenty of people lust after me, both wives and husbands. It's all part of being alive, the lusting for and being attracted to other people, whether they're married or single. It's those animal spirits in us, Reverend. Because, that's what we are, animals not plants. God made us human, so he must have known this was going to happen. Like I already admitted in commandment six, I never did it with any happily married people. On this one, number nine, I plead no contest, nolo contendere, and throw myself on the mercy of the court. That means you and God, Reverend Digby...Reverend Digby, you still with me?"

"I'm bleeding. I think it's coming from my eyeballs. I need to find a handkerchief or a towel to soak up this blood."

"Well, lucky for you we're practically done here, Reverend, because number ten is a no-brainer. Everyone covets what they don't have and other folks do have. I see men with all the money, all the power, all the rewards this life has to offer and of course I want to take it away from them. They don't deserve any of it. I want to give it all to the women in this world who truly do deserve these nice things, these trophies that reward our pursuit of happiness. How could God possibly believe that we would not covet what our idiot neighbor has and we don't? When I finally meet up with God, oh and I will, Reverend Digby, this is the first question I want answered."

"Mary, I think you have to talk with the Bishop. He sometimes does private confessions. Your sins are far beyond anything I am trained for. I'm feeling feverish, yet I have chills at the same time. I'm dizzy and I'm still having trouble breathing. My legs are completely paralyzed now."

"Alright, Reverend Digby alright, sounds like you've had enough. I do feel better, lighter, getting all of this off my chest. Now circling back to number five, Thou Shalt Not Kill, I know that's a big one..."

"Do you hear church bells, they're ringing louder and louder? Can you hear them, Mary?"

"No, I don't hear any bells, Reverend Digby. Besides, we don't have church bells in Roma anymore. I got rid of them, they made too much noise early in the morning. Like the poem says, perhaps they toll for thee...Now, getting back to, Thou Shalt Not Kill, they all deserved it anyway."

"ALL! Did you say all?"

"Yes, I said all...four men who were complete assholes who bullied and disrespected everyone they had ever met, especially the women. They needed killing so I killed them, and this world's a better place because I did. It was easy Reverend Digby, easier than you'd think. Like all bullies, they were afraid of meeting the bigger bully, of being dominated like they'd done to others. So that's what I did. I broke them down mentally and dominated them right down to their last suffocating 'why me' breath. Bully's always turn out to be the biggest pussies. They always want you to choke them. I just did what they begged me to do and said to hell with the safeword...I gave them one brief moment of ecstasy followed by three prolonged minutes of agony. Sounds like a fair deal to me."

"So yes, Reverend, I guess most people leave here to meet their maker having broken most of the commandments, except for number five, Thou Shalt Not Kill. I stepped over that line, more than once and I'm not apologizing for it. If God is going to put me in this Purgatory of a world, and don't tell me this isn't the pure definition of Purgatory, Reverend Digby, if God's going to surround me with men who are

154

monsters, men who attack innocent women and children every single day and night, then I'm going to do his work and bring retribution. In all honesty, Reverend Digby, since that's what I'm being here today, completely honest, I'll probably have to kill again and again until things are made right."

"Mary, my organs are shutting down. I've lost all my senses. I think I've urinated myself. Please stop talking and call me an ambulance. Maybe they can save me, but I doubt it. I promise not to say anything, Mayor Mary, but we both know there's no penance I can give you for what you've told me here today. I will pray for you, and I will pray that your entire confession does not haunt me for the rest of my life. Go now Mary, and never set foot in this church, or in any church again."

"I am getting ready to go, Reverend. Pretty soon, I'm leaving Roma, or what is left of her anyway. I'm moving out to L.A., Hollywood, California. There are some fatcat movie producers out there who need to be tamed so some important movies can get made about the power of women, instead of the silly comic book fluff they're putting out now. I believe God wants me to go to Hollywood as his avenging angel executive producer.

"Please, do give God my best, Reverend Digby, and tell him I look forward to meeting him. But not too soon, I've still got a lot of work to do down here. Tell him I have many questions that need answering. Oh it's two-thirty, my ride, Chief Ridley, should be waiting outside now. Me and the Chief, we go way back, Reverend Digby. I told you I had a brother, didn't I? He's my twin brother in fact, and we are very, very close. I just thank God for never giving Moses that eleventh commandment, **Thou Shalt Not...**"

## TEN YEARS AFTER

"He saved all those kids that night. He did. You have to give him that."

"I don't have to give him jack shit...he was an asshole. Always was, always will be, and besides, he didn't save that one kid, not the fat retard with the earphones."

I watch them every Friday, two guys barely in their fifties. They sit at that same corner table, staring out the window at our rusting brown bridge, drinking their cheap whiskey and arguing about how it happened. Ten years after, and it's still all anyone in this poor excuse for a town can ever talk about, because it's the only big thing that ever happened here in Babylon.

"You just never liked him because he left, he got out of here."

"Yeah, but he came back, didn't he. Assholes always do. If everything is so much better out there, why do they always end up coming back?"

I can hear it all loud and clear from my perch at the bar, even with my back to them. I watch in the mirror above the bar. I see and hear everyone from my spot. Those guys talking, they're our two most high and mighty townies, the brains and the brawn of this forgotten backroad hideaway. Together, they resemble Laurel and Hardy, the big fat guy and the little skinny guy from those old black-and-white movies who were always making plans that never worked out. That's Harry and Conrad.

Kenny Conrad, the gorilla-looking guy, hates everyone who's not from here, anyone who doesn't walk and talk just like him. People just call him Conrad. He's a genuine moron who's never traveled more than fifty miles away from this town, and never will. His only claim to fame, which he still talks about all these years later, goes back to his high school football glory days when he was captain of our mediocre team. Because of his elephantine size he was offered a scholarship to the state university, only 48.2 miles away. He was back here two weeks later, claiming a knee injury in summer practice cost him his scholarship. But the simple truth is, Conrad just wasn't good enough. Those other guys hit way too hard, so he packed his bags and left his dorm room in the dead of night on the fourth of July, not saying a word to anyone. He's been working for the town ever since, paving roads and fixing potholes mostly, still wearing his letterman's jacket every day. When he gets drunk, he'll rub his knee and start talking about the college ball he never played. We've hated each other ever since grade school when we got into a fight in the schoolyard. He knocked out my two front teeth, so I went crazy and kept banging his head on the ground until three of his came out. Conrad hasn't had anything to say to me ever since that day. He kept on being a bully, just not around me.

"He got what he deserved, that's how I see it. Never fit in around here anyway, that whole family. Why do you always gotta make him out to be some kind of hero? I don't get it. Any one of us could have gone stumbling down there and probably done a better job."

"But that's just it, Conrad, we didn't. He did." Harry Hancock's voice always sounds high-pitched and squeaky when he talks through that microphone he holds to his throat because of the lung cancer. It gets garbled when he's had a few drinks. Already tonight, Mayor Harry's had more than a few. Harry found out last month he needs a new kidney because his old one just doesn't work anymore, and they can't find anyone who's a match who wants to give, or even sell him one. Ever since he got the bad news, Harry's been repenting, sorry for all the shitty things he's done over the years. It's funny how people find God and want to be forgiven when they know they don't have much time left. But hey, they did what they did, it's too late to change that.

"We are the choices we make." He taught me that, the guy they're still talking about, my best friend since childhood, Simon.

The Hancock family owns this town—the land, the businesses, the real estate—pretty much everything, even this place, Harry's Bar & Grille. Harry Hancock, who looks even smaller and almost disappears when he's sitting next to Conrad, the monolith, is this town's mayor for life, or at least it seems that way for as long as he's been mayor. The more excited he gets, the higher his voice goes, and Harry tends to get excited easily. By last call, it sounds like there's a bird chirping around the bar, but it's only Harry the last of the Hancocks, telling everyone how good they have it here in Babylon.

Nobody can really disagree with him. If you want to work, eat, or drink in this town, and who doesn't, you better stay on Harry's good side. It's a solid scam he's got set up— we all work for Harry, he pays us money, not very much, which we spend at his businesses, mostly at this bar. It's the Capitalist hustle at its local best. We are all trapped in this vicious cycle of daily survival while little Harry Hancock keeps spinning the wheel with his not-so-invisible hand.

Problem is, Harry's got no kids, never tried to get married, or even go out on a date, so far as I know. What happens to this town when Harry's voice squeaks no more, and the wheel stops spinning for all his townie dependents? We're going to find out soon enough.

"That fat kid was his brother, you know that, Conrad. I can't tolerate you still hating him after all this time, especially tonight. He came back to take care of his brother when his mother got sick, and there's honor in that. Whatever happened between you two is past and done. Nobody cares anymore, probably never did. So just let it go, or at least shut the hell up about it."

"I'm just saying, he never liked it here anyway. He made that clear, so it's no big deal he's gone. As far as taking care of his brother, he did one hell of a job at that, didn't he."

Conrad knows it's time to back off when Harry's voice hits its highest squeaky pitch. Even an idiot knows never to bite the hand that feeds, and like all pigs at the trough, Conrad feeds a lot.

Harry pours himself another whiskey from the bottle on the table. Conrad puts out his glass for another. Harry just pushes the bottle over to let him pour his own. He's had enough of Conrad already, and the night is so young.

"Feels like he's still here every time we look out at that bridge. I see it all so clearly. See him running across the ice trailing that fire hose, all of us laughing at him. I remember he didn't even have a hat or coat on, no gloves either. Just slipping and sliding on that ice while we sat up here drinking and doing nothing. I mean, I still don't get it...we're good people, we work hard, go to church on Sunday, sometimes...what happened that night?" Harry's hand shakes as he raises his glass.

"Ice was too thin. Nobody should have been out on it, not in the middle of the river like that. Sometimes you just have to let things happen, and that's what we did. He's gone, we're still here—I call that a win-win situation. Why keep beating yourself up about something that happened so long ago? You tell me to let things go, you should let things go, Harry, especially this one."

"You really don't get it, Conrad. That's the saddest thing. This town hasn't been the same since that night. It won't let us go, not ever. People don't come to Babylon anymore because of what happened here."

Conrad pours two more shots. They sit in silence watching the sun set behind our rusted old bridge, built during the Depression by men who just wanted to work, feel productive and build things that mattered. That feeling is gone now. Our infrastructure is falling apart, and nobody seems to care. People just want to keep things the same and not lose what little bit they have. Joseph told me that's when we lost our humanity around here, the day everyone started acting so desperate and began looking out only for themselves. I wonder if it's like that everywhere, or just here.

Harry Hancock knows what I know. This is the night, February 25th ten years ago today. It happened just before sunset, that's when everything changed and time stood still for everyone here in this bar tonight. But not for Joseph. He saw that moment perfectly for what it was and jumped right in.

"Colder than a Catholic girl on prom night, that's what it is out there. Why the long faces, boys? Who died?"

Steve Satchmoski, our volunteer fire department chief, breaks their silence from the next table. Everyone calls him Satchmo because he used to play the trumpet way back in middle school. He was horrible at it. l remember Satchmo as that gangly boy who liked to smoke in the woods and start forest fires when we were kids. He always looked funny when he'd come loping out of the smoking trees like something was chasing him, trying to get away from being blamed for his latest blaze. Now all these years later, Satchmo is our fire chief who spends most of his time putting out forest fires that seem to start all by themselves over in Roma. Funny how most people end up going full circle in life.

Conrad's happy to have Satchmo in their conversation. Combined, they never broke a thousand on their SATS back in high school, so together, they take intelligent communication to a whole new level; they lower the bar.

"Harry's sitting here eating himself up about the accident, like we all should have done something about it. I say better him than me...I mean us. Today's the day you know, anniversary day February 25th, ten years ago today. Sun's going down, so it was right about now." Conrad checks his watch and pours himself another shot of anesthesia.

Chief Satchmo looks out at the bridge. "Shit, I forgot it was today. All day long I've been thinking something happened, but I couldn't come up with what it was. Look, there's the bus going over the bridge now, just like then. It's kind of eerie. But hell, we were all drunk, we couldn't have done anything."

We watch in silence as the little red bus makes its way across the rusty brown bridge spanning the frozen river, then disappears into the gray shadows of winter's twilight. As I look in the mirror, I can see everyone in the bar is watching the bridge. Their eyes look dead and their faces like skeletons as they sit frozen in place, just like that night. Even me, here I am at my same bar stool watching, drinking and remembering.

"If he had just waited, I could have organized a proper rescue effort, instead of running down there half-cocked and fully crocked. We just needed more time, that's all. We would have done something, there just wasn't enough time." Chief Satchmo pours another whiskey and slumps back in his chair muttering on about how there's never enough time.

Harry Hancock, still looking out the window, squawks back at him. "He was waving at us to come down there and help. You know that, Satchmo. We all saw him and just didn't care. Or even worse, we wanted them to die. It's why you're here, why we're all here tonight. Don't tell me you forgot this was the day. You're not that ignorant. Close maybe. We'll never forget this day, it's our recurring nightmare. We could have made a difference, maybe even saved them. But instead we just sat here drinking and laughing at them. You made a choice not to help, we all did. Stop making excuses, or you can stop drinking my damn whiskey."

Chief Satchmo stands up and wanders away to the other side of the bar, just like in his younger days when he would flee the scene so he wouldn't get blamed. These days he's still running away from the truth. Conrad jumps right in where Chief Satchmo left off. They always did make quite the tag team. Who do you think was right behind Satchmo when he would run out of the woods acting all innocent and smelling like smoke?

"It's not my nightmare, Harry. Shit, I don't even dream anymore. I barely sleep. Usually I just pass out for a few hours, wake up around three and go back to work, where I sit in my truck waiting for the rest of these assholes to show up. I'd kill for a good night's sleep, Harry."

"That's my whole point, Conrad. We already did the killing."

A quick check of the bar shows all the pillars of our dwindling community here tonight. It's like taking roll call back in school. Standing over by the jukebox are the Miller brothers, Tyler and Teddy, along with their fellow motorhead Wally Fox. As always, they're arguing about what song they want to play next as Warren Zevon howls out his last war cries on "Werewolves of London." The three of them run our local gas station, which of course, Harry Hancock owns.

Sitting across the bar from me are the Blake sisters, Betty and Bunny, who claim to be twins but don't look anything alike, except for their large breasts. I guess they could be fraternal, but Bunny looks Hispanic and Betty could be Swedish, so go figure. They swear they're twins though, always have. Betty and Bunny work at our town clerk's office collecting taxes and issuing licenses. I remember how they couldn't stop laughing that night watching those kids walking the wrong direction on the ice, away from shore. Betty, the Swedish twin, fell off her barstool she was laughing so hard. Between the two of them, they've probably had sex with everyone in this bar at least twice. Even me, I am sorry to admit, but never Harry. I think he's the only virgin left in this hole of a town.

Every Sunday, though, you'll find the Blake sisters singing their impressive lungs out, front row center in the church choir, acting like Jesus is their special boyfriend. They've even come up with their own original interpretation of the Bible, which they like to quote as they're seducing and bedding their mostly married men. Funny how everyone takes what they want from the Bible and swears God commanded it.

Our local police force, all three of them, are here tonight sitting in the far corner over by the pool table. Chief Tillman and his two deputies, Billy Taylor and Jimmy DiGeorgino, stop in every Friday for Happy Hour. Makes me wonder, who exactly is keeping us safe if our entire police force is sipping umbrella drinks at Harry's Bar & Grille? They were all here that night too, watched the whole thing happen right there from that back table. Chief Tillman never even reached for his radio to call Roma for first responders to help get those kids out of the bus and off the ice. He just sat there watching, enjoying the show along with the rest of our town leaders, as the thin ice cracked and gave way around the bus. Our police chief kept on sipping his whiskey-sour as the cold grey waters surrounded those kids on that little red bus, their innocent faces looking out from the windows, unable to understand what was happening to them and why. Tillman knew right then what the outcome was going to be, and he seemed just fine with it. His over the hill deputy dogs did too; officers Taylor and DiGeorgino were cheering the loudest of everyone. Those three put a whole new twist on 'to protect and serve', just not during Happy Hour.

"That's not what happened, and you know it, Conrad. Their bus hit the bridge railing then fell onto the ice, but it didn't break right through. It sat there for almost twenty minutes before going under. You, me, hell any of us had plenty of time to get down there and help. He actually did. We all saw the same thing, so why try to change the facts. Who are you fooling anymore? Nobody here, not tonight." Harry was getting revved up.

"I'm not trying to fool anyone, Harry. I didn't say there wasn't time. What I mean is there wasn't any time to organize a safe rescue. Shit, even more people could have died instead of just him and that idiot brother of his. Look around here, Harry. You see your real friends, the people who matter in this town. We're all still alive, and that means something too. What if even one of us had died trying to save a bunch of retards. Now that would have really been something to cry about. That's all I'm saying."

"Our town did die, Conrad. Everyone who watched it happen and didn't do a goddamn thing to help died that night, and that's everyone here tonight. All present and accounted for. Seeing those kids go home in that little red bus, crossing the bridge every night, that's to remind us of what happened. We get to come here every Friday for Happy Hour and drink to forget. But we never can forget. Why do you think you can't sleep anymore? Poor Conrad, if only it could be high school forever." I'll bet Conrad had that exact same thought every day, lots of times.

Babylon is built along the banks of the Winooski river, so pretty much every house and building looks down the hillside to the river. Harry's Bar & Grille sits on top of the hill, just a few hundred yards from the bridge, which used to look pretty all lit up at night. Now the lights don't work anymore, and the bridge is just a run-down reminder of what happened ten years ago today...

That night, we were all sitting here as usual, nursing our cocktails watching the sun disappear behind the bridge. There's not much else to do in Babylon on a Friday, or any other day for that matter. I remember, Simon was sitting right next to me when it happened. It all did happen fast, that much is true. Soon as Simon saw the little bus go off the bridge and hit the ice he took off. He said, "HOLY SHIT," and jumped off his bar stool. I couldn't take my eyes off the bridge and what was happening down there. The bus must have hit a patch of ice and skidded right through the railing. It dangled from the bridge for a few seconds then took a nosedive onto the ice, stood upright for about a minute then fell again, landing on all four wheels. I remember thinking that was good, everything would be alright because it landed the way it should, like it was safely parked near the middle of the frozen river. The only crack in the ice I could see was the hole made when the bus crashed down from the bridge. It didn't look that bad, just one little hole.

We'd already had a few pops, so Simon was a little drunk when this happened. Maybe that helped, maybe it hurt, I'll never know, but it didn't stop him from jumping right into action. He grabbed the firehouse hanging on the wall by the extinguisher, ripped it right off the nozzle on the way out. Nobody else even noticed him, or me. They never did anyway, but that night they were all standing by the windows watching the show, having too much fun to give a shit about us. I can still hear "The Devil Went Down To Georgia" playing on the jukebox, the perfect song for what was happening in Babylon that Friday night.

When he appeared outside the bar, slipping and sliding down the hillside, everyone started hooting and hollering, especially Harry who was cackling the loudest with his microphone turned up full blast. It was quite a sight. Simon must have figured the road would take him too long, so he took the express route down and just let the icy hill do all the work. He flew through some bushes, bounced off a few tree trunks, then launched ten feet into the air at the river bank, making a hard-landing on the ice with a full face-plant. But he kept holding on to that fire hose. I can still see him clearly as he turned around, looking back up the hill at the bar, motioning for us to follow him down there to help.

Conrad broke the silence that night. "What now, asshole? What you gonna do with that busted hose?" That got a big laugh, especially from the twins, Betty and Bunny, who were standing on top of the bar to get a better look at what was happening.

"He's such a damned fool. That ice is gonna break under him. He's just too fat to be out there. Look, Bunny, he's waving at you. He wants you to tie him up with that hose like you do to Conrad."

"Conrad ties himself up, Betty, it saves time. Look, there goes Ettie Hollinger. I didn't know she could run so fast. Did you, Betty? Hey Ettie, didn't you forget something? What about the retards?" Bunny got a big laugh as Ettie Hollinger, the bus driver, managed to climb out and took off running for shore, leaving her dependent passengers behind and still belted in their seats.

I could see cracks starting to lengthen around the bus, like a spider weaving its web. Joseph met Ettie in the middle of the frozen river and tried to grab her as she ran by. But Ettie stiff-armed him like a fullback running over the last defender between her and the end zone. Everyone enjoyed seeing Ettie send Simon five yards into the air, landing him flat on his ass. That got an even bigger laugh.

"Good hit, Ettie. You know she's not gonna stop running until she gets home, locks the door and pours half a bottle of bourbon down the hatch." Chief Satchmo used to be married to Ettie, so he knew her habits well.

What Simon did next was brilliant, I thought. I still do wonder if he had a plan in his head soon as he saw what happened, or did it just come to him when he got down there. He must have grabbed the hose because he knew the ice was going to break. The clock was ticking, it was just a matter of time. He only had about a hundred feet of hose to work with. What he did was to tie the hose to the bridge railing, the part that was hanging down about twenty feet away from the bus. Just as he was tying it off, the left side of the bus cracked through the ice.

"It's going in, she's going down. Hope you can swim, dimwits." Chief Satchmo's joke didn't get as much laughter. Everyone knew then, the little red bus was about to break through the ice and sink down thirty feet into the river's powerful current. The bar went completely silent, but still nobody moved to help. Not them. Not me. Not a one of us.

When Simon got there, water was already gushing up and making its way into the bus as the ice cracks stretched out from the widening hole where it first hit. He came up with that first kid, then went back in and came out with the second. The bar crowd watched and counted as one by one he led those kids out of the bus and over to the hose dangling from the bridge. He looped the hose around each of them and must have told them to hang on, help was coming. They did. They stayed on that hose for a while. I still wonder if Simon really believed help would come. He kept disappearing back into the bus, which was halfway under by now, to come out with another kid. Watching him, it seemed like it took an hour to get those ten kids out. It didn't, but everything happened so fast, every single second lasted too long as clearly, time was running out.

There was only one kid left in the bus, and I knew it was Thomas, Simon's brother, the one Conrad always called the fat kid. That was the moment I finally said fuck it, I'm going to help him. I grabbed my coat, ran out the door and took the same downhill route Simon did, hitting the same rocks, bushes and tree trunks. I think I caught a little more air off that last jump at the riverbank and probably landed a little bit harder. But I got there quick enough.

It may have happened ten years ago, but everyone here tonight looks so much older, maybe fifty years older. When I look around me all I see is dead people with empty eyes and lost faces. Our whole town, like our bridge, is rusted and broken down beyond repair. We sit here every Friday night drowning ourselves in Harry's cheap liquor, not just trying to forget what happened but trying to invent reasons why we let it happen. Our punishment is being forced to relive that ugly moment when everything changed in our little town...changed in me, forever.

I see now, they've never forgiven me for trying to help Simon, even though I turned out to be too little and way too late. Nobody talks to me anymore. They act like they don't even see me, like I'm one of those untouchables in India who everyone ignores and avoids. They treat those retarded kids the same way when they see them around town, at the bowling alley or the pizza parlor. Those kids are constant reminders of the night they just don't want to remember, but can never seem to forget.

By the time I finally arrived on the scene, he had gone back inside the bus and been there for a few minutes. I remember thinking as I was running on the ice, Simon should be coming out by now–where is he? The kids were trying to un-loop themselves from the hose as the ice cracked all around them making that loud snapping sound ice makes when it breaks off. The moon was full and unblocked. The whole scene was lit up for the fools on the hill watching from Harry's Bar & Grille. By now the bus was three quarters filled with water, but I knew there was still time to get them out. I couldn't understand why Simon was still in there. Maybe he hit his head and I was going to have to carry him and his brother out. They were both bigger than me, I couldn't see how that was going to happen. The entire front part of the bus was submerged now with only the back part still visible on the ice. I dove in and swam through the front door, pulling my way seat-by-seat in the icy water to reach the back of the bus. There they were, the two of them just sitting strapped in, like they were about to go on one of those Disney rides at Magic Mountain. They were holding hands, Simon and his brother Thomas, holding hands and singing like they always did when I would see them walking around town together. The water was rushing in and there wasn't much time left. Simon looked at me and spoke calmly.

"Thanks for coming, Jacob, I knew you would. But we're doing just fine here. Me and Thomas, we're going on a little trip together, going to see our Mom. You take care of those kids, and get the hell out of Babylon just like we talked about. I mean it, Jacob. You're a good old soul. Now get out of here, before it's too late."

His brother, Thomas, just kept smiling and saying, "MaMaMaMa." I could feel the bus sliding and knew they weren't coming with me, so I touched the top of Simon's head for a moment; I don't know why, I just did. Then I pushed backward into the water swimming toward the front door. I cleared the door just as the bus got sucked down into the current beneath the thick surface ice. Their faces went right by me as I swam in the opposite direction, Simon waved as they passed. Then he smiled and hugged his brother closer. I watched as the little red bus caught the current down river, like it was flying, never even sinking to the bottom, just floating away until I couldn't see it anymore. I felt that same current pulling me away from the hole in the ice, away from the escape hatch I needed to reach. I pushed upward with what little air I had left, up toward the moonlight shining through the opening which was beginning to darken and close over.

Reaching for the light, I grabbed on to the cracked ice and pulled myself up. The jagged surface ice broke off in my hands, sending me back under with bleeding hands, and weaker now in trying to fight the current. Again, I swam straight up to the light, knowing this would be my last chance to escape the river's pull. I reached up, and this time a big chunk of ice broke off like a shard of glass, enlarging the hole which now took on the shape of a giant toothless grin, taunting me as I sank down again for what I was sure would be the last time. As I gave up and surrendered to the current, something dropped past me. It was the hose Simon had tied to the bridge. Somebody threw me the hose. I grabbed on and pulled myself upward, hoping someone was pulling from the other side. With no air left in my lungs, I was inhaling the water entering through my nose. I was drowning.

When I broke through the top, I sucked in all the air I could and kept throwing up water. With each deep breath I took, more water came out. I felt hands on my back, pulling me as I clutched the hose, clinging so desperately to the lifeline I thought would never come. Then everything stopped, all fell silent. I was looking up at a beautiful starry night as somebody dragged me away from the hole, away from what I had accepted was going to be my watery grave.

I looked up and saw Big Barry and his buddy, the one we called Elvis, two of the retarded kids from the bus. Barry always wore a cowboy hat, which somehow he still had on. Elvis, wearing his black leather jacket with his hair slicked back, actually said to me, "Thank you very much." They were laughing as they dragged me by my feet along the ice, my bloody hands leaving a red trail across the frozen river.

Just up ahead, I could see the others from the bus walking together, holding hands and singing some song I didn't know. They were going the wrong direction, walking away from the closer shore, away from safety, trying to cross the river and get back home just like they did on their bus every night. I knew the ice formed even thinner in the middle. They were going to break through again walking in a group like that, and I had nothing left in me to help them.

I took a breath and yelled out, loud as I could. "Barry, Elvis, you gotta turn them around. We have to go the other way or we're gonna fall in again."

"We're going home now. It's time for supper and we don't wanna be here anymore. It's too cold. Not nice here." Barry let go of my foot and my leg dropped hard to the ice. He walked off toward the others. I couldn't move and didn't feel anything when my leg hit the ice. I lay on my back and looked up at the winter night sky. The stars seemed so close. Just past the stars I could see three tiny blue-green-red dancing lights, and then they were gone. I could hear the kids just up ahead, but I couldn't move. I wanted to go to sleep. I called out to them one last time.

"Hey, you're going the wrong way. The ice is breaking. We have to go back. If you come here and get me, we can all go to my house and I'll make you spaghetti and meatballs for dinner. We'll get dry and warm and eat lots of spaghetti." I couldn't move but I could still talk, and that was the best I came up with. What kid doesn't like spaghetti and meatballs on a freezing cold night like this? It sounded good to me.

After a few minutes of laying in silence, I knew I had to get myself moving. No help was coming. I turned over on my stomach and began crawling back toward shore. There wasn't much time. I had to get off the ice before frostbite and hypothermia set in. As I crawled, I could see the silhouettes up on the hill, watching, laughing and hating from Harry's Bar & Grille.

"Spaghetti and meatballs, you promised. Can we have some garlic bread too?" It was Elvis, and with him were the other kids, cold and wet and shivering. Elvis and Barry grabbed my feet and started pulling me back to shore as the others followed. "Which house is yours?"

"Just walk toward where the bridge begins, and I'll take you home. I'll get all of you some nice warm blankets. We can have cookies too. I have some. Hey Barry, you did good, you're a real cowboy. Elvis, you know you're the coolest. Thank YOU very much."

Barry howled at the moon. Elvis just curled his lip, pointed at me and nodded his head. I could hear sirens approaching and saw flashing lights coming down the hill on the bridge road. Finally, some help from Roma. Ettie must have called it in from home after a few shots of bourbon gave her enough courage to do the right thing, or more likely, to cover her ass.

Those kids never did get that spaghetti dinner I promised them that night. The paramedics stuffed me into an ambulance and rushed me off to County Hospital over an hour away. They had me on life support for the whole trip and said at one point I was dead for over two minutes before they shocked me back. It took three shocks at high voltage to revive me. I was treated for frostbite and extreme hypothermia and ended up losing my two middle fingers, one on each hand, and two toes on my right foot. The doctors said I was lucky. If it wasn't for all the ice and freezing water keeping everything in place, I might have lost my whole right hand, the cuts were so deep. Doctors have funny ideas about what 'lucky' is.

It wasn't until two months later that they let me out of the hospital. While I was in, they gave me so much morphine I slept most of the time. I miss the morphine, but I'm glad to be walking, more like hobbling, and out on my own. First thing I did when I got out was to show up at the kids' group home with more spaghetti, meatballs, pizza and garlic knots than they could even eat. Who opens the door that night? It was Big Barry of course, wearing his new cowboy hat. He grabbed me in one of his big bear hugs and squeezed until I almost dropped all that food. I cried just a little bit and whispered in his ear, "Thank you, Barry. Thank you for everything."

Now I sit here tonight, surrounded by the desperate faces of Babylon's aging has-beens and clueless never-weres. I can see death all around me, the slow excruciating funeral march of these people who were always too afraid to leave this town and now realize they never can. They have been sentenced to this prison of nothingness with no chance of reprieve or parole.

Tonight's the night, though. Down at my feet, my hockey bag sits, half open and ready to make some serious noise. I've got enough firepower in there to blow all these people to hell and well beyond kingdom come. I brought the arsenal...my MAC-10, two Bushmaster semi-automatic rifles, one sawed-off shotgun, my 9-millimeter pistol and Dad's Colt .45 pearl handled cowboy six-shooter, the only thing he left me when the lung cancer finally got him. His new wife took everything else, even the house I grew up in. But Yee-Hah, I got the Colt.

It's all planned out, I've been sitting here thinking about it for years, ten years to be exact. That's why I rolled the dumpster up against the back door before I came inside tonight. I don't want any one of these townie hypocrites missing out on the fun, or getting out of here alive. Now there's only one way out, through that front door which is where I'm going to set up shop when I start shooting. Chief Tillman and his deputy dogs won't be a problem. Harry never lets them wear their guns into the bar, especially when they're drinking, which is all the time. Their guns are out in the patrol cars, where our police force ought to be. But they go first, just in case.

I won't shoot to kill quickly, that would be way too easy on them. The idea is to make them suffer and die slowly so they can think about what is happening to them. I can never understand why in the movies they always kill off the villain so fast at the end, with one clean shot or quick explosion, after he's been torturing, killing and hurting good people for the whole movie. The bad guy, or bad girl, gets off easy with a quick death. Who doesn't want a quick, painless death? Well, not in my movie. Nobody dies easy tonight.

It's time. I put on my white cowboy hat, Barry's old one that he gave me for the ambulance ride to County Hospital that night. I zip open the bag. This is going to be too easy. I know there are no heroes in this whole town, and certainly not in this bar. I figure there's maybe fifty people here tonight, give or take. I have way more ammunition, over 500 rounds, much more than I'm going to need. I'm aiming for the stomach and lower body on everyone except the Blake sisters, they get buckshot to the bosom since that's the body part they're most proud of. The motorheads, always standing over by the jukebox, they'll probably try to hide behind each other. I'll just mow through them with the MAC-10 as I go by, so I don't have to waste too much time. Satchmo, our pyromaniacal fire chief, gets the 9-Mil to his kneecaps so he can't run away, and one to the groin for good measure, just for being an asshole.

I'll save Conrad the gorilla and Harry the squealer for last. I figure they'll be hiding underneath their table by the window, waiting for it all to end so they can sneak out the back door. I thought of them with my dumpster move. I'm saving the Colt .45 for them, groin area again, plus a kidney shot for Harry, and a couple of knee-cappers for Conrad so he finally will have that knee injury he's been talking about for so many years. I even brought my holster to make it look true-cowboy. Everyone else just gets a quick spray from the MAC so they can lay in their blood and remember why this is happening to them while I tend to the rest of the garbage. Simple plans are the best, and now it's time to put this one to work. It shouldn't take too long, five minutes maybe, just like that night ten years ago today. Then, I'm out of here, finally.

I strap the bag across my chest and reach for the MAC-10, feeling for the cold trigger and pushing the clip into place. The backup clips are already in my belt along with my 9-Mil. As usual, nobody notices me as I slide down the bar toward the door. I'm invisible to them. Tonight, that's for the best.

Betty and Bunny climb up on the bar and start dancing like they always do when they've had a few too many, which is always. Won't they make easy targets. Chuck Berry belts out "Johnny B. Goode", while the motorheads argue about what song they should play next. Harry and Conrad sit silently staring out the window at the rusty old bridge, as I pull the MAC-10 from my bag.

"Jacob, you're listening but still not hearing. You don't belong here anymore." I hear his voice clear as ever. That's Simon's voice, talking to me just like when we used to sit at the bar and he was telling me about his travels and adventures, and all the places I needed to go see for myself.

178

"They're not worth it, Jacob. Besides they're already dead. They can't leave here. You can go, Jacob, to a better place, so get out of here while you still can."

I look down the bar from where I was sitting, and see Simon in his usual spot clear and even shining, his brother, Thomas, sitting next to him with that big smile on his face. They're looking right at me and even though they're ten feet away, I can hear Joseph clearly, like he's whispering in my ear. I'm not afraid, I'm happy to see them. Then just as I move over to get closer, they're gone, vanished right before my eyes. I let go of the trigger and let the MAC sink back inside my bag. I sit frozen. That really just happened, but I'm the only one who saw him, heard him, and I think Thomas actually whispered my name, *'Jacob'*. I'm feeling a little bit dizzy and sick to my stomach, like I'm seasick. My whole body feels paralyzed, just like it did that night when Big Barry and Elvis were dragging me across the ice and I couldn't move. I know I have to get out of here or I'll get sick right on the bar. Then they'll notice me for sure. I zip the bag closed and stagger out the door.

The crisp night air hits me like the pure oxygen they gave me in the ambulance. I breathe in deeply as I make it to my truck. I hear his voice again, but this time I can't see where he is. I gun the truck and head down the hill to the bridge so I can cross over.

"It's time to go, Jacob. You don't have to be here anymore."

My plan was to shoot up the bar, kill every last one of them, then get the hell out of this sorry excuse of a town. I'm all packed and ready to go. Everything I need is right here in the truck. Just two duffle bags, a suitcase, and oh yeah, my hockey bag with all these guns. I'm keeping the Colt, he's the only family I have left. The rest I figured I'd drop in the river on my way out of town, on the other side of the bridge where everyone does their ice-fishing. Thought I'd let the current take the guns where they can't do any harm and never be found. I figure I'll head north to Canada, go get a job working on the oil sands up there in Alberta. That's what Simon did to get out of here. It was his first stop. He worked as a welder. I've been practicing my welding and I'm pretty good at it now, even got certified.

After that, I plan to keep heading north, go see those Northern Territories, maybe prospect for gold in the Yukon. Then, it's over to Australia, just like Simon did. I'm going to follow in his footsteps, close as I can. He said making money along the way is easy. You just take the jobs nobody else wants because they are either too dangerous or actually require some skill to do. Live simple, and when you have enough money saved, just move on. Seems like every night we talked, it ended with Simon saying to me, "Keep moving forward, Jacob. All this life is about is trying to move forward, even if it's just a little bit at a time."

I always knew I was going to drop the guns in the river from Conrad's fishing hut. Seems like a good idea to me. I leave my truck running on the bridge road so the heat stays on, and I walk out on the ice. No way I'm taking my truck out there like those idiots do when they're ice-fishing. You hear stories on the news all the time about trucks breaking right through and going under, but still those morons do it every weekend. With my bad luck on the ice, I don't want to risk it. I'll just dump these guns, get on down the road, and never look back.

It's like a village out here with all these fishing huts. Ice-fishing is just a silly reason for guys to get shit-faced and get away from their wives and kids for the weekend. It's not so different from regular fishing, except you freeze your ass off and usually end up passed out on a cot in the freezing cold, surrounded by a bunch of other guys, instead of being at home in a cozy bed next to your hopefully warm wife. Hmmm, it seems like a peculiar way to spend time.

There it is, Conrad's hut. Leave it to that asshole to make it easy to find. He's painted it red and orange, our old school colors, with his football number '56' emblazoned in neon orange on the front door. I can feel under my feet the ice is thinner than usual for this time of year. Doesn't matter to me, I'll just make a quick deposit and get off this slab lickety-split, quick as I can. I should be well north of here before the big thaw. I don't even like being out here now. Ever since that night, I stay away from the river as far as I can.

I kick-in Conrad's door, before I notice it had no lock on it. Feels good to do it anyway. Inside, I am immediately confronted by a life-size poster of Conrad "The Killer" in full uniform wearing number '56' and ready to make yet another game-saving tackle, which he never even did. I remember in senior year, our team went four wins and six losses, and that was our best season in the four years he played. Pretty awful, but that never stopped Conrad from basing his entire life on it. People are good at forgetting what really happened; you just have to give them time and keep repeating the lies.

Suddenly, I need to take a piss, and Conrad's hero-pose seems like the natural target. I arc it high to get on his face, don't want to miss that helmet. Now he looks like he's playing his big game in the rain. I might as well get some satisfaction out of this final mission. Besides, it's a good way to say goodbye to the big asshole. Hell, we'll always have ice-fishing, Conrad.

My hockey bag won't fit through Conrad's fishing hole, which is fine by me because I'm still itching to take a shot at something tonight. I could drop the guns individually, but there's no fun in that. This is a job for my Bushmaster, so I pull her out and start firing around the hole to make it larger. It looks like that grim toothless smile again, the same one I saw grinning at me from up above in the ice that night. Then, so long as I'm shooting holes, I fire a few rounds at Conrad's football poster, and at his cooler, and his cot, then I just shoot up the whole place because it feels so right. I stop firing only when the magazine empties. It's then I hear the cracking sounds. I know that noise, like the sound dry wood makes when you're splitting logs. It's the snap and crackle without the pop. But it's coming from outside; I don't see any cracks in here besides the big hole I just made in the ice. I drop the Bushmaster back in the bag, zip it up and toss my guns into the dark gaping hole, which now I can see has a few thin cracks extending from it, or to it, I can't tell which. My bag floats in the hole for a few seconds then disappears, probably down river a bit, then to the very bottom. There's lots of stuff down there, it must look like a junkyard by now. People are always tossing things they don't want into this forgotten river. Nobody cares anymore.

I'm officially out of here. As I turn for the door there's another big crack, and just like that, the entire hut lurches forward, sliding the doorway under water, blocking my exit. Maybe I shouldn't have kicked it in. Now the door's half above the ice and half submerged as water floods in, much too strong for me to swim against. There's no room to get out with the doorway wedged on the ice like that and the water gushing in. My head won't even fit through. The thing about ice fishing huts is there's no big windows; they're usually built solid enough to stand up to the cold and wind you get at night. I know right away my only chance of getting out is going to be after the water fills the hut and starts sucking it under, then, maybe I can swim up through the hole I made. At least the opening is plenty big enough to climb through, I made sure of that with my Bushmaster. I can't believe this is happening again. This damn river just won't let me go. I'm thinking, 'maybe I shouldn't have left my truck running'.

I sit back on Conrad's cot and wait for the water to fill up. There's really nothing else to do now, just stay calm and wait for my moment. The hut shifts again, standing straight up like the Titanic before its final plunge. I hear more ice cracking. Then my hockey bag comes gushing back into the hut and hits me in the chest. I guess it never even made it to the bottom, just got turned around and came full circle back up through the hole. No matter how hard you try, some things you just can't get rid of, they just keep coming back at you.

Strange how I'm not scared, not even a little bit. I know what I must do and feel everything's going to work out. I'm just sitting here, waiting. The hut is almost filled up to the top with water now. I'm taking my last few deep breaths before I go under for the swim back up. Just as I'm getting ready to push off, I hear his voice again, calm and clear like it always was.

"Now it's your time to leave here, Jacob. You're free to come with us. We'll show you what comes next, things we never even imagined. How could we have living here? You're ready, Jacob. It's your time."

I can see them now, the both of them. Simon with his brother, Thomas. They're shining and beautiful, smiling at me just beyond the doorway, as the ice hut surrenders to the river's pull and disappears beneath the dark water. The strong current immediately carries the hut downriver, away from my escape hatch, the one I will never reach. I breathe in the river's water. It tastes sweet and fills my lungs. I feel the river taking my body, as I leave it.

There's no pain, just acceptance. I take Simon's hand, then Thomas's. We hug tight, becoming one, and leave the river. I'm better now. I feel warm and safe and know that I'll be alright. I'm with them, and they're taking me to a better place than here.

I see big beautiful stars welcoming us. Those three blue, green and red shimmering lights I saw that night ten years ago beckon up ahead. I understand everything now...I am home.

# ROMA HAS FALLEN

"Going-out-of-business sale, Rufus? You're actually closing up shop? No more Reardon's General Store in Roma? No more Rufus? We'll have to drive all the way to Babylon, or even Trusca, just to get a tank of gas or buy some milk and bread. Say it ain't so, Rufus."

"Sorry to say, but it is so, Chief. There's just not enough folks living in Roma anymore to keep a general store open. It's a sad day for me too but also a special one. It was on this very day, one hundred and fifty years ago, on a snowy, cold March morning that my grandparents opened the doors and served their first customers at our general store. They thought it would never close, that it would stay a family business forever, passed on down through the generations. I hate to be the one to end it, but times have changed. Roma's become one of those drive-thru towns where no one stops for very long anymore, just the skiers when we have good conditions, and they get less every year."

"Well, we've had a bunch of the white stuff this winter, that's for sure. Seems like it's been snowing for five months straight. It's almost April and here comes another blizzard. What are you going to do with yourself, Rufus?"

"Don't know yet, Chief. Hate to leave Roma but feels like it's the right time to go."

"Where though? Just don't say Florida. Lots of retired cops move down to Florida and end up dying seven months later. I think it's those early-bird dinner specials that gets them. You're just not supposed to eat dinner at three o'clock in the afternoon."

"Or maybe it's just the boredom that gets them, Chief. Florida's pretty damn boring, and hot all the time too. It's not a natural living situation for human beings. Nah, if anything I'm heading north, and then west over to British Columbia. I always wanted to see Vancouver Island. Maybe I'll go live there for a while and see if I like it."

"But that's Canada, Rufus. That's a whole 'nother country. Can you do that, just go and live there?"

"Oh yeah, there's a bit of paperwork involved, but as long as you're spending money and not causing any trouble, they let you in, and even treat you nice."

"Well, at least now I know how to get everyone in town to show up at one place—just hold a Fire Sale. There's more people here than at any town meeting lately. I better get back to the station, Rufus. Mayor Mary's pissed off about something. Always is. Drop in before you go to say goodbye."

This is how it used to be, people shopping and talking and just enjoying each other. Folks took pride in Roma, pride in our schools. We were that golden city on the hill, the place where everyone lived the good life…

"How much is the beef jerky today, Mr. Reardon?"

"Billy Burkenstock, my favorite truant, and you're actually going to buy something this time instead of just making it disappear. Everything is half off, so if it says three dollars, as that package does in your hand, well you tell me how much it is, Billy."

"Buck fifty a pack, now that's a deal, Mr. Reardon. Finally, I can afford something in here. I'm taking ten of the beef teriyakis. That's fifteen dollars, done deal. And Mr. Reardon, I'm sorry you're closing the store. I always liked coming in here. It felt more like home than my own home ever did. I think Roma's going to miss you."

"It's time for me to move on down, I mean on up the road, Billy. But thank you."

"Me too you know. I swear, I'm out of here the day after graduation next June. That's a little over a year; I can make that. Then I'm moving down to Boston, going to study computers and astronomy. Ivan said I could stay with him until I get all set up."

"That's real good news, Billy. Listen to Ivan, he's a wise man. Turns out just about everything he said was going to happen to Roma ended up happening. He knows things you don't, and that's called wisdom."

"I know a few things too. That's why we like to talk. But I do like listening to Ivan. See-Ya, Mr. Reardon, and thanks for all the jerky and stuff."

"Samantha's playing up a storm out there. Seriously Rufus, the more she plays the harder it snows. Are you paying her to conjure up this blizzard so everyone has to stock up on wine and beer? Pretty smart thinking, Rufus."

"No Coach, Sam just showed up out of nowhere and started playing like always. I have noticed, every time she puts on her red beret and starts talking like she's got a band behind her, people stop what they're doing and just enjoy the show. Can't blame the snow on Samantha though, it's been that kind of winter. Look at them dropping money into her violin case. Kid knows how to make a buck better than I do."

"I heard you sold the store for a pretty good price, Rufus."

"Yeah, I did alright, Coach. But promise not to tell anyone, they're putting a Taco Bell in here, knocking down the general store to build a Taco Bell. Hated to do it, but the money was just too damn good."

"All those years we fought off the barbarians, and Taco Bell breaks through the gates. I always thought it would be a McDonalds. I do like their cheeseburger and fries. You know the others are going to be right behind them now. How could you let them in, Rufus?"

"Had no choice, Coach, only had the one offer. It was either take it or burn the place down for the insurance money. Don't think I didn't consider it. Anyway, fast food is about all anyone can afford these days. You'll be alright. McDonalds will be here soon enough, and then Burger King, then Arby's. Once the gates are open, they'll all come in. Who knows, maybe we'll even get an Applebees."

"I'm leaving too, Rufus, going back to New York City. I got an offer last week from a small college to coach women's basketball. Seems like the right time to go. I have my eyes on a certain point guard I want to recruit in a few years. She has 'championship' written all over her. Is the beer half price too? I'm going to need more than a few to get through this storm and then the next. When is it going to stop, Rufus?"

"Everything's half off, Coach, especially the beer. Wine too. That much I know. The storm? That's anybody's guess. Roma's drinking tonight and we'll pay the price tomorrow. Stringer, keep your monkey away from the bananas. Bubba's not even allowed in here. I still have a strict no monkeys allowed policy in Reardon's General Store. You know that, Stringer. Tell Bubba to stop looking at me like that or I'll have him arrested again."

"What about primates in general, Rufus. Are we still allowed in?"

"Well hello, Katie Konklin. Now it's a party. You are always welcome here. These others, I'm not so sure about."

"Quite the sale, Rufus, it's like you're giving it all away. I saw the cars lined up and thought there must be an event happening at the general store that I just didn't hear about."

"Nah, it's just the demise of another Roma institution. I was going to tell you, but things got hectic. Figured I'd have my final sale before all the looting started. I'm leaving town tomorrow, gonna drive across Canada and maybe stay for a while. I was gonna stop by in the morning before I left."

"I'm happy you're going but sad you're leaving, Rufus. I get it though, there's nothing here anymore except memories and disappointments. What happened to this golden town, Rufus? What happened to all of us? I feel like we failed somewhere along the line, but I can't remember when."

"Time did it to us, Katie. It gets everyone sooner or later. We were the right place at the right time for a while. We had our run. But things changed. People lost interest in being that special place. Taxes just keep going up until nobody can afford them anymore. Our once excellent school is going further downhill every year because nobody wants to pay for it. There's not even enough money to fix the roads, and a mountain town needs its roads fixed every year. It's not our fault Katie. People just moved out and moved on to the big cities where there's still some jobs, not good ones but a few anyway. You really should get out of here too, Katie, on to your next adventure. Still plenty of life left in you."

"Well thank you, Rufus. I think I'm going to take that as a compliment. Why don't you stop by for a cup of coffee and some chocolate chip cookies before you hit the road. We both deserve that."

"I'm leaving early, Katie, gonna try to beat the worst of this storm."

"The earlier the better, I'll see you in the morning, Rufus. Now I'm getting busy with this half-off sale before Stringer's monkey chews everything up."

"Stringer, what did I tell you about Bubba? Keep your crazy monkey outside where he belongs."

I look around my great grandparent's store, my grandparent's store, my parent's store, my store. I see the people of Roma—my neighbors, my friends, my classmates—all desperately grabbing for food and drink they don't really need but feel they must have to make it through the night into tomorrow. I've known these people all my life and they are good people. I love these people, and I will miss them.

Our faces tell the tragic story of Roma's fall. We watched helplessly as our economic system, capitalism, fell apart and failed us all—except of course the rich people, the capitalists, who fled Roma years ago. We listened to our supposedly elected political leaders lie to us about how things were getting better and opportunity was coming back to Roma. We listened because there was no other hope on the horizon. Then finally, we gave in and gave up. We allowed our high-minded principles to become hollow platitudes. We embraced everyday hypocrisy as Roma's new normal for accepted behavior.

It is one minute before midnight now. My Subaru is all packed up and ready to go, when I am ready to go. I'm in my massage lounge chair in front of the dwindling fire, pouring the last bit of expensive Cabernet I was able to salvage from what was once my family's proud contribution to the town of Roma—Reardon's General Store. As I listen to the wind whisper, and watch the snow fall silently, I drift off into a deep sleep, accepting that all is as it should be. I will move forward now. Roma is no more.

I open my eyes at first light. It's best to just get going. If I'm really leaving, then leave, no long goodbyes or second guesses. I'll send Katie a postcard from Vancouver Island. That's for the best. I fire up the Subaru and pull out of my parking lot into the heavy snowstorm. Just beyond the store's entrance stands Katie Konklin, my very own girl next door with suitcase, coffee and cookies in hand.

"I knew you'd never stop by, so I hoofed it over here. Got room for one more in that old jalopy of yours, Rufus?"

We kiss as we should have kissed so many years ago and begin our journey together. As we drive down the mountain road one last time, we pass Samantha playing her fiddle. This time I believe I can see her Strange Family Band if only for a moment, then they disappear into the blizzard. Further on down the road, I look in my rearview mirror. I see Roma fading away, but a ghostly image of the shining star she once was. I miss her so.

## AT THE END OF THE DAY

"It's going to be a cold one tonight, Elvis. You want some of this?" Jake hands me the joint. He shouldn't, but he always does.

"I can't believe they're still up there. We need to set up for dinner soon. Hey, don't smoke the whole thing, Elvis. That's powerful stuff."

People like to call me Elvis because of my sideburns and how I slick back my black hair so I look like him. Elvis was the coolest, nobody's ever been cooler than him. Jake's our chef. He likes to do two things—cook food and smoke weed. Jake smokes a lot of weed. He says it makes him a better cook. Maybe so, he makes delicious food.

"I keep telling you, Elvis, little hits are better. You have lungs like a sperm whale, kid."

We're watching the sun set over the lake. I like the colors, how the orange runs into the red with the blue and gray trying to catch up, like a sailboat race.

"That is definitely enough smoke for you, Lil Elvis. Maybe you ought to go check on them. Bring them some coffee or something. Shit, it's almost six o'clock for God's sake."

"If you want me to, I will Jake, but I don't think it's a good idea. They told me to close the big doors and said they would come down when they were finished. Mayor Mary said nobody should interrupt them. But I'll just tell them Jake sent me and how you want them out now so we can set up for dinner..."

"Jeez God no, Elvis, don't say that. What are you trying to do, get me fired, again? We'll give them another fifteen minutes before you go a-knocking on those closed doors. That's all I need, the High and Mighties complaining I gave them the bum's rush. Definitely don't need that."

"Hey Jake, I always want to ask you. Why do you call them the High Mighties?"

"Because they think they're better than everyone else, Elvis. There's a lot of self-righteous piety sitting up there eating my beef stroganoff and enjoying your Cobb salad. High and Mighty Hypocritters is what they are."

Jake always says words I don't understand when he's smoking. But he gets pissed off when I ask him what they mean, so I stopped asking. I just know he doesn't like the High Mighties. He doesn't think they're nice people because they do mean things to everyone else and never say they're sorry.

The four High Mighties Jake hates the most are Harry Hancock, Babylon's Mayor with his squeaky microphone voice; Mary Yeldir, the Mayor of Roma, the next town over from us who likes to boss people around; Reverend Digby, who preaches to Roma and here too because we don't have churches anymore in Babylon; and Chief Ridley, who does everything Mayor Mary tells him to do and follows her around like a hound dog

They meet here every Friday afternoon at three o'clock sharp for their late lunch in the private dining room at the top of the stairs. For the last four years, I've been their waiter, the only one allowed in and out during their private lunches. Mayor Mary says she likes me best because she doesn't have to worry about me telling anyone what I heard, or anyone believing what I told them. Jake says she's the meanest of all of them, and the other High Mighties are afraid of her. I think he's probably right, Mayor Mary is a hard-headed woman.

I like it when people call me Elvis. Jake says I look like Elvis before he got famous. I don't like it when people call me the retard. My mom says I was born with the extra chromosome which makes me think and sound different from others. Most people are cool and don't make me feel bad, but some people go out of their way just to call me the retard. Mom says they make fun of me just so they can feel better about themselves and their own shitty lives.

"Look at that, Jake, over there to the left. See that purple sky?"

"Holy shit, Elvis. That's a golden eagle flying across your purple sky. They're rare around here anymore. Give me the damn joint back. Don't give me that shit you forgot you had it. You never forget anything, Elvis...tell me, what was the Final Jeopardy question last Monday, not this week but last week?"

I think for a while and then I see it in my head, "...the category was geography."

"Oooh, I hate geography. Never did any good at it in school. The nuns used to beat the shit out of me for not knowing where the Tropic of Cancer was, or what countries made up the Balkan states. I still don't know where that Cancer is, or who the Balkans are. I knew you'd remember the question, Elvis, you never forget anything. Now hit me with it for all the marbles, what was the damn question?"

"I don't have any marbles, Jake, but the question was, this country's Cape Agulhas separates the Indian and Atlantic

Oceans. Alex Trebek gives you ten seconds to think about it and write down your answer."

"I don't even need ten seconds, Elvis. I got this one. Let me see, you have Europe and Australia and China...it could be Russia."

"Buzz...your time is up, Jake. What is your final answer? And it's not any of the ones you just said."

"It's not? Alright then, I'm going with Mexico. They're always separating shit from Mexico."

"No, I'm sorry Jake, the answer was not Mexico. Not even close. The answer was South Africa. Cape Agulhas is in South Africa where the Indian and Atlantic Oceans meet."

"Shit, Elvis, you don't have to rub it in. I hate geography. Fuckin nuns, they ruined my love for geography."

Every Friday for the last four years now, Jake and me sit out back here between shifts, watching the sun set over the lake before we get ready for dinner. Usually by now, the High Mighties have cleared out, but not today...

Last month I watched a movie on HBO that gave me this idea. When I'm not at work here at the restaurant I'm always watching TV and movies. There's not much else to do in Babylon, even if you're not retarded. This movie was called, The Wannsee Conference. It was all about how these Nazi officers and political leaders got together for a big fancy lunch so they could plan how they were going to get rid of all the Jewish families and Jewish business people in Europe. I mean really get rid of them, by killing them all. They were eating a big buffet lunch and drinking fancy wine while they talked about the best ways to kill off all the Jewish people. It got me to thinking how these Nazi generals and politicians acted so sure of themselves with how they were going to hurt and kill millions of people, they reminded me of our High Mighties upstairs the way they talk at their lunches.

I told Jake about the movie and he agreed with me. That's exactly what our High Mighties do up there every Friday while they eat and drink too much. They decide who will live and who will die by picking who gets the good jobs, and who gets the money to live nice. Jake says they make sure no outsiders get any of the good stuff so there's more money and power for them and their friends...just like the Nazis did in Germany. Mayor Mary even has a list of people she keeps, people she doesn't like and who she tells Chief Ridley to keep an eye on. Harry Hancock just sits there drinking and mostly agrees with everyone, especially Mayor Mary. At the start of every lunch, Reverend Digby raises his glass of red wine and makes the same toast, "At the end of the day, we must protect what truly belongs to us, the real Americans...here's to We The People."

They all bang forks on their glasses when he says that. Jake says I'm the only guy in Babylon, or anywhere, who they would ever let hear them say that kind of stuff. Usually they just think it or whisper it, but they never say it out loud in front of anyone else. Except me.

"Hey Elvis, it's definitely that time. Go on upstairs and knock hard on those closed doors and tell those fucking hypocritters we need the room. Oh yeah, and do not use my name. I mean, this shit's getting ridiculous. Another hour and we might as well bring them dinner too. What the fuck?"

"Alright Jake, but I think I did hear the door lock behind me when they closed it."

"Not good Elvis, not good."

Jake takes one last hit off the joint and snuffs it out. He heads back into the kitchen to get dinner ready, and because he doesn't want to be around in case there are any problems with our special guests. I'm left alone in the dark, once again, staring out at the towering mountain that separates our sad town of Babylon from the forgotten town of Roma, and the rest of the outside world. It feels so peaceful now, the way life always should be. There are just a few colors left from the sunset as the wind whispers my name through the trees...Elvis, it's time to go upstairs, time to rock this jailhouse, Elvis.

"At the End of the Day", I've heard them say it so many times at their lunches. I've listened to the politicians, the lawyers and the bankers say it on TV when they are trying to explain why they did what they did. I don't understand many things, but I do understand "At the End of the Day." It means people will do anything, all the mean and horrible things they can think of, just to keep what they have, to keep their power, to keep things in place. To them, everything must stay the same "At the End of the Day." Nobody and nothing else matters, just like in the Nazi Wannsee movie. I see it so clearly now. Why doesn't everybody else?

I kept thinking when I was watching that movie, what if someone had heard their plans and knew those Nazis were gonna do horrible things to good people? What if someone decided to do something about it? Maybe they could have poisoned the food and wine and killed all those Nazi leaders right then and there to put a stop to it. Would have been easy for a waiter to do. Waiters are invisible, nobody even notices us. Chief Ridley always likes to tell the same joke about me. He says I look like the head waiter at the Last Supper. I'm never sure what he means by that, but today he's right about it being the last supper part, or last lunch anyway.

It was really pretty simple, any idiot could have done it, even a retard. First, I cut up a bunch of the poison mushrooms I took from the woods near where Jake grows his weed. He showed me the poison mushrooms so I would never eat them. Jake thinks I like to walk around the woods eating things. I don't. But I did pick a bunch of those mushrooms yesterday and put them in the Cobb salad I served the High Mighties today. When I left the room after serving their lunch, I locked the big oak door from the outside and kept the big key in my back pocket.

It's now or never. I feel good as I climb the long dark stairway, slowly reaching the top step. There are no sounds coming from inside the dining room, just silence. I unlock the big door and turn the shiny brass doorknob. I am ready for what is waiting for me on the other side because I know I did the right thing. I will not run away, Elvis never runs away. I will tell Jake, the police and everyone else with suspicious minds the whole truth and nothing but.

Just like every other Friday, I served the High Mighties their lunch and went downstairs when Chief Ridley told me to leave the room. I will also tell everyone the things I heard the High Mighties say. The mushrooms were poisonous? I don't know anything about that. I picked them myself to use in my Cobb salad, the one I make every Friday for the last four years. How could anyone blame me? Don't be cruel, I just don't know any better.

I guess at the end of the day I am not the retard. I am Elvis, doing what needs doing, my way. So, don't get all shook up. Thank you very much.

end--copyright Jameson Flynn 2018

www.ingramcontent.com/pod-product-compliance
Lightning Source LLC
Chambersburg PA
CBHW070343260626
47160CB00011B/2700